BEOWULF

GOLD EDITION

EDITED BY
ADAPTIVE READER

TRANSLATED BY
FRANCIS BARTON GUMMERE

ISBN: 979-8-8692-6217-2 (paperback)

Ebook: 979-8-8692-6218-9

INTRODUCTION

Welcome to Adaptive Reader, your portal to the captivating world of literature, tailored to fit your unique reading abilities.

In today's fast-paced and diverse learning environment, we believe in the power of personalized learning experiences. That's where the concept of leveled reading comes in, and why we, at Adaptive Reader, have dedicated ourselves to offering a broad collection of classic novels at various reading levels. Our mission is to make the joy and benefits of reading accessible to everyone.

THE BENEFITS OF LEVELED TEXTS

So, what exactly is leveled reading? It's an approach that matches students with texts that align with their unique reading abilities. This ensures that every reader is challenged just the right amount - enough to grow, but not so much that they feel overwhelmed or frustrated.

For students, this means you'll engage with texts that stretch your reading skills while keeping the experience enjoyable and manageable. You'll gain confidence as you successfully comprehend each level and feel motivated to explore more challenging texts as your reading skills grow.

For teachers, Adaptive Reader provides a valuable tool to support differentiated instruction. You can assign the same novel to your entire class while ensuring each student reads a version that aligns with their reading level. This allows all students to participate in class discussions and activities, fostering a more inclusive learning environment.

For parents, Adaptive Reader offers a supportive tool to encourage your children's reading journey. As your child progresses through the different levels of a novel, they'll not only enhance their reading skills but also develop a deeper love for literature.

READING ACROSS MULTIPLE EDITIONS

All of our leveled novels include passage markers that correspond to the same content across every one of our editions. This means that passage '62' in our silver edition contains the same themes and plot elements as passage '62' in our original edition.

For teachers, this means that you can say "let's look at passage 35 together. What is the author trying to tell us here?" and all of your students will be reading the same content — but with vocabulary and syntax that's adapted to their reading level.

Our online reading tool, available at www.adaptivereader.com, gives students and teachers free access to the original text with passage markers. We encourage teachers to include close readings of the original text as part of their coursework, giving all students exposure to the rich original syntax and language of these exceptional authors.

THE POWER OF LITERATURE

At Adaptive Reader, we are committed to helping everyone experience the power of literature. So whether you're a student diving into a classic novel, a teacher looking for flexible resources, or a parent seeking ways to support your child's literacy, Adaptive Reader is here for you.

We invite you to embark on this exciting literary journey with us. Enjoy the world of stories, characters, and ideas that await you in our collection of leveled novels. Happy reading!

PRELUDE OF THE FOUNDER OF THE DANISH HOUSE

1   BEHOLD, we have heard tales of the mighty kings,
The spear-wielding Danes, in days of old,
And the honor they achieved, their glory won!
Often Scyld, the son of Scef, fought valiantly
Against countless enemies, from many tribes,
Impressing the nobles with his might.
Once abandoned, he was now rewarded by fate:
He flourished and grew in wealth and power,
And the people who lived by the sea paths
Heard his commands and presented him with gifts.
Truly, he became a great king!
In time, he had a son,
A child born in his grand halls.
He was sent by heaven itself,
To bring comfort to the suffering people,
Who had longed for a strong leader.
The Lord blessed him with remarkable fame.
This Beowulf, son of Scyld,
His reputation echoed throughout the Scandinavian lands.

It is the duty of a young man to show loyalty
To his father's friends, through gifts and kindness,
So that in his old age, they will stand by him,
Should the need for warriors arise in times of war.
Through noble deeds, an earl gains respect
In every clan, earning honor and glory.
And so, brave Scyld embarked
On his final journey, guided by God's protection.
His loyal clansmen carried him
On a ship adorned with rings, strong and ice-covered,
And gently placed him on the boat's breast, the breaker-of-rings.
Near the mast stood the powerful leader. He brought many treasures
from distant lands, which were loaded onto the ship.
I have never seen a ship so splendidly equipped
with weapons of war and armor for battle,
with breastplates and blades. On his chest, there lay
a heap of treasure that would soon travel
far across the sea with him.
No fewer treasures were placed
by the noble lords than those
who had sent him away long ago,
when he was just a helpless child.
They raised the banner high above his head,
a golden flag. They let the waves take him,
gave him to the ocean. Their hearts were heavy,
filled with sadness. No one can truly say,
no inhabitant of the halls, no hero on earth,
who carried that precious cargo.

BOOK 1

3   Now Beowulf stayed in the city of the Scyldings,
a beloved leader, ruling with fame
amongst the people, since his father had passed
away from the world. Then arose an heir,
proud Healfdene, who held in his life,
wise and strong, the joyful Scyldings.
Then one by one, he had children:
Heorogar, then Hrothgar, then brave Halga;
and I heard that Hrothgar's queen was
the dear companion of the Heathoscylfing.
Hrothgar was given such glory in war,
such honor in battle, that all of his kin
obeyed him gladly, and his band
of young comrades grew great. He thought
to have his men build a grand hall,
a majestic mead-house, bigger
than any ever seen by men,
and within it, he would distribute everything
that the Lord had given him,

except for the land and the lives of his men.
I heard that the work commanded
was great, spread across many tribes
around the world. It was completed quickly,
the noblest of halls, standing proud:
He named it Heorot, its glory spreading
through many lands. He did not forget his promises,
giving out rings as treasure at banquets.
The hall stood tall, with wide gables,
waiting for the fiery surge of battle.
But it was not long after that day
when the father and son-in-law stood in conflict,
filled with warfare and renewed hatred.
An evil spirit held envy and anger
in his dark dwelling.
He heard the sounds of merrymaking
echoing in the hall every day.
He heard harps playing, and clear songs sung
by a skilled singer. He sang about
tales from the earliest times of mankind,
how the Almighty created the earth,
with beautiful fields surrounded by water,
placing the triumphant sun and moon
to bring light to the people,
and adorning the earth with plants and trees,
creating life for all
living beings who breathe and move.
The clansmen lived in happiness,
leading pleasant lives, until someone
began to bring about trouble, turning it into a hellish place.
This terrible monster was called Grendel,
a mighty terror, living in the marshes and wilderness.
He was a descendant of the giants.
For a time, he had avoided this unfortunate creature

since the Creator had exiled him.
God's sovereignty punished the killing
to avenge Abel's murder by Cain's kin.
His feud came to a bad end, and he was driven far away
from the sight of men because of the slaughter.
From Cain's bloodline, came a terrible breed:
giants, elves, and evil spirits,
as well as the giants who once fought against God,
who grew weary over time; but they received their just reward!

BOOK II

5   HE WENT out searching at nightfall
        for that proud hall and paid close attention
        to where the Ring-Danes had gone to rest,
        after their revelry had ended.
        Inside he found the noble warriors
        asleep and unbothered by sorrow.
        The did not expect any human suffering.
        The unholy creature, fierce and greedy,
        quickly grabbed thirty of the thanes,
        rushing away.
        He was ager to return to his lair to slaughter.
        As dawn broke and day began,
        the presence of Grendel became known to men.
        After the festivities came cries of despair,
        a loud morning sadness. The mighty leader,
        the excellent prince, sat there, troubled,
        grieving for the loss of his thanes.
        Once the trail of the fiend had been discovered,
        the cursed spirit. The sorrow was too cruel,

too long, too repulsive. The respite came quickly,
Yet as night returned, the ruthless killing resumed.
He cared nothing for the feud or his crimes,
steadfast in his guilt. Those who sought
rest in distant rooms, far from the terror,
where they bedded down for the night,
were easily found. When the evil was shown,
when it was seen for certain, with undeniable proof,
the hall became the source of the hate.
Those who escaped the fiend's grasp
stayed far away and kept themselves safe!
In this way, the beast ruled and raged,
destroying all, until the noble building stood empty
and remained that way for a long time.
For twelve years, the king of the Scyldings
endured great trouble and countless sorrows.
News spread
among the people, revealing the reality
In sorrowful songs, the constant torment
of Hrothgar by Grendel was sung,
his deep-rooted hatred, the murders and massacres
that lasted for many years, an endless feud.
He refused to negotiate with any of Daneland's nobles,
There was no peace or compromise with gold.
The wise men knew they would never
receive payment from his fiendish hands.
The evil one lurked and ambushed both young and old,
bringing dark shadows of death, chasing them,
Or tempting them into the misty moorlands.
No man can say where these Hell-Runes dwell.
The hater of men, a loner,
Continued with acts of horror and suffering.
He ruled over Heorot, the grand golden hall,
in the gloomy nights, and the prince could never

approach his throne or find joy in his hall.
This sorrow was deeply felt by Hrothgar,
causing heart-wrenching misery. Many nobles
gathered and sought counsel on how courageous men
could confront this terrifying menace.
They made vows at their heathen altars,
offering sacrifices, and pleading
for the soul-slayer to grant them relief
from the pain inflicted upon their people.
Their heathen practice was rooted in their hope,
thinking only of Hell in their minds.
They knew not the Almighty,
the Judge of Deeds and fearsome Lord,
nor did they ever consider Heaven's protection,
the Wielder of Miracles. It is a pitiful man
who willingly embraces harm and hatred,
without seeking favor or change.
He always waits. But fortunate is the one
who, after their last day, can go to their Lord,
and find friendship in the loving embrace of the Father!

BOOK III

8 THUS THE SON OF HEALFDENE,
    continued in rage and sadness,
    as the woe of these days consumed him.
    No wise men could ease his sorrow,
    for the pain was too great,
    a terrifying and enduring torment,
    that burdened his people, worst in the night.
    News of Grendel's actions reached
    the great warrior Hygelac's loyal follower,
    the mightiest man of valor in our time,
    strong and majestic.
    He commanded a ship to be prepared,
    declaring that he, the king of battles,
    would go far across the sea,
    seeking the noble monarch who needed aid.
    Prudent people did not blame
    the prince's decision to undertake the journey,
    though they held him dear.
    They encouraged the hero and celebrated signs.

And so, the courageous one gathered
a group of the best warriors among the Geats.
With fourteen men, he embarked on the ship,
tested sailors leading them to the borders of the land.
Time passed and the ship floated,
bobbing in the water. They climbed aboard,
ready for battle, as the waves churned,
mixing sea and sand. The sailors carried
their shining armor and weapons on the boat's deck.
With a determined push, the men set off,
guided by the willing wind, directing the sturdy craft.
The ship sailed across the waters,
swift as a bird with foamy wings,
until, on the second day, it reached
the curved prow's intended path.
The sailors caught sight of land,
shimmering sea-cliffs, towering hills,
and wide headlands. They had found their safe haven,
and their journey had come to an end. Swiftly then,
The warriors of the Weders' tribe stepped onto the shore,
Mooring their sturdy ship, creating a clash of armor
And the sounds of battle equipment. They thanked God
For their safe passage across the treacherous sea.
On the cliff above, a guard from the Scylding clan
Observed as they carried their gleaming shields
And made ready their weapons. He was filled with wonder,
Eager to know the identity of these men.
He quickly rode his horse to the beach,
A loyal servant of Hrothgar. With a powerful hand,
He shook his spear and began a conversation.
"Who are you, armed men,
Clad in mail, who have brought this mighty ship
Over the ocean to our shores?
I am a guardian, trusted to protect this sea-border,

Unless any enemy fleet should bring harm to the land
Of the Danes. Never before have I seen
Strangers so at ease...
Yet, it is clear that we didn't know you'd be joining us.
Among all the warriors
In this world, I have never seen one as great as
The hero among you, dressed in splendid armor!
But if his appearance is any sign,
He is not a mere follower, but a worthy leader.
I urge you to reveal your origins and purpose,
So you will not be mistaken for spies
In the land of the Danes. Now, as travelers from afar
Who have sailed the ocean, take my advice:
The sooner you inform me of your homeland, the better."

BOOK IV

10 To HIM, the most esteemed among them replied,
the leader of the warriors unlocked his voice:
"We are kin to the Geatish clan,
and loyal companions of Hygelac. My father,
a noble prince named Ecgtheow,
was well-known in distant lands.
He departed from this world after many winters,
honored still by wise men across the world.
In a spirit of loyalty and respect for your lord and liege,
we have come here, to the son of Healfdene,
the protector of his people. Please, advise us!
We have an important mission to the mighty ruler,
the lord of the Danes. I do not believe
that anything should be kept hidden. We have heard--
you may know whether it is true--of a fearsome
and dark monster among the Scyldings,
a wicked creature that appears in the dark of night,
inflicting terror with unmatched rage,
spreading hatred and death. I wish to offer Hrothgar

my assistance with a brave and noble soul,
so that the Wise-and-Brave may overcome his enemies.
If it is fated that an end to these horrors will come,
that a cure will follow this cruel contest,
and that the boiling waves of troubles will calm,
then afterwards, Hrothgar can live free of anguish.
But if not, he will suffer in sorrow,
while that unmatched house stands atop the hill!"
The guard of the coast, still on his horse, responded,
fearless and devoted to his clan: "A noble warrior
must know how to carefully separate
words from actions, if he intends well.
I understand that this group is kindly disposed
towards the master of the Scyldings. So, march on,
holding your weapons and following the path I show you.
In the meantime, I will instruct my men
to guard your boat in case any enemies come--
Your new ship,
rests upon the shore as it faithfully awaits
the return of those beloved warriors
who will sail it gently
to the land of the Weders,
where destiny will guide them to aid and protect
against the ravages of war."
They set off on their journey, leaving the boat behind,
Anchored firmly,
a wide vessel. The boar symbols gleam
Along with the golden accents,
shining brightly and steadfastly guarding
the warrior within, as the heroes march onward,
eagerly hastening until they catch sight of the hall,
with its broad gables and dazzling gold.
It is the most magnificent hall in all the world,
where Hrothgar, the renowned ruler, resides,

and its radiance illuminates the distant lands.
The valiant shield-bearer proudly points out
the awesome place, and instructs them
to go straight towards it. Then he turns his steed,
brave and courageous, and addresses them:
"Now it is time for me to leave from your company.
May the Almighty Father protect you with grace and mercy,
keeping you safe in your endeavors. I shall go to the sea,
and stand guard against any hostile warriors."

BOOK V

12 THE STREET WAS ILLUMINATED by bright stones, guiding the way
for the group of warriors. Their shining armor
was hand-crafted and strong. As they marched,
the steel rings on their gear sang out,
creating a melodic rhythm. They arrived at the hall,
weary from their journey across the sea,
and placed their bucklers and shields along the wall,
before taking a seat on the benches. The clanging breastplates,
weapons of war, were stacked,
and the spears of the seafarers stood together,
made of sturdy ash wood with gray tips;
a well-equipped band of warriors! A proud warrior
inquired about their origins and kinship.
"Where do you come from, carrying polished shields,
gray armor, and intimidating helmets,
with a multitude of spears? I am Hrothgar's messenger,
and never have I encountered such powerful strangers.
It is clear that you seek Hrothgar not as outcasts,
but as valiant heroes of great courage!"

The fearless warrior, Beowulf, responded with confident words,
a proud earl of the Weders. "We are of Hygelac's lineage,
companions in battle. My name is Beowulf.
I am here to deliver my message to the son of Healfdene,
your lord and master, the mighty prince.
If he is willing to grant us an audience,
we come to greet him with respect."
Wulfgar, leader of the Wendles,
known for his strength of mind, courage, and wise counsel,
spoke:
"I will gladly inform the king of the Danes,
the friend of the Scyldings, about your request,
the renowned prince who holds the title of Ring-breaker.
I will swiftly return with his response."
To the worthy king's delight, Wulfgar hurried
to where Hrothgar, with his white hair, sat
surrounded by his loyal earls.
Standing by the Danish king's side, the loyal thane
spoke to his respected ruler:
"Great lord, there are men from distant Geatland
who have journeyed across the vast oceans to see you.
Their leader, Beowulf, stands tall and proud with his brave
companions.
They humbly request an audience with you, my liege,
to speak of their purpose. I beg you, gracious Hrothgar,
to grant them this favor and listen to their words.
They are dressed as true warriors, deserving of our admiration.
Their leader, especially, has shown great courage in guiding
them here."

BOOK VI

14   Hrothgar, the king of the Scyldings, replied:
        "I remember him from his younger days.
        His father was Ecgtheow, a respected man,
        who was given the only daughter of Hrethel the Geat.
        Their brave son has come here to find a loyal friend.
        Sailors who delivered my gifts to the Geatish court
        have told me that he has the strength of thirty men,
        fierce and skilled in battle.
        It is by God's mercy that this man has been sent
        to the Danes of the West to face the terror of Grendel.
        I plan to reward him with gold for his courageous intentions.
        Quickly, go and invite them to come before me,
        the clan of his kinsmen; tell them that they are
        welcome guests among the Danish people."
        Wulfgar went to the hall's entrance
        and delivered the message:
        "My master, the king of the East-Danes,
        sends this message to you.
        He recognizes your noble lineage and courage,

and welcomes all of you here, across the sea!
You may come dressed in your armor,
and greet Hrothgar with your helmets on.
However, leave your shields and weapons behind
until your meeting is over."
Beowulf and his brave companions rose,
accompanied by their loyal men who guarded their gear.
Following the herald, they made their way to Heorot's roof,
and the hero, wearing his shining breastplate and war-net,
spoke:
15　"Hello Hrothgar! I'm Hygelac's relative and follower.
I've become famous in my youth! I've clearly heard
about Grendel's actions in my homeland.
Sailors say this hall, the best of buildings,
stays empty and unused when the evening sun
sets. My people, brave and wise, advised me
to come to you, Hrothgar, because they know
my strength and courage. They've seen me
come back from battle, covered in my enemies' blood,
after I defeated five of them, and in the sea,
I killed sea-monsters at night, in danger and distress,
avenging the Weders' troubles, defeating the fierce ones.
Now, I want to face the cruel monster Grendel
in a single fight! So, I ask you, Hrothgar,
leader of the Shining-Danes and protector of the Scyldings,
to let me and my men, this brave group,
clean Heorot. I've heard Grendel doesn't care
about weapons; so I'll fight him without
sword or shield, just with my hands.
Let fate decide who survives. If Grendel wins,
he will fearlessly eat my Geatish warriors
in this golden hall, as he has done before.
You won't have to worry about burying me,
for he will have my body, soaked in blood,

to take back to his home in the swamp.
If I die, send my armor, the best one
protecting me, to Hygelac. It's an excellent piece,
made by Wayland, and it was Hrethel's before.
Let fate happen as it must."
He will fearlessly eat, like he has done so many times before,
my bravest warriors. So there is no need
to conceal my head. I will be his,
covered in blood, if death must claim me.
He will carry my bloodied body as his prey,
devour it,
staining his den with my life's blood in the marsh.
There is no need for you to prepare food for me anymore!
If fate decides that Hild takes me,
send word to Hygelac to decorate me
with the finest armor, a treasured heirloom from Hrethel
and the craftsmanship of Wayland. Destiny will unfold as it
must.

BOOK VII

17 HROTHGAR SPOKE, leader of the Scyldings:
"For defensive fight, my friend Beowulf,
you have come to help and save us.
Your father sparked a feud in battle
when he killed Heatholaf with his hands
among the Wylfings. The warriors of the Weder clan,
afraid of the consequences, banished him.
Fleeing, he sought safety with our South-Dane people,
crossing the ocean to the land of the Honor-Scyldings,
when I began my rule over the Danish people.
In my youth, I ruled this vast kingdom,
this stronghold of heroes. My older brother Heorogar was dead,
Healfdene's son, and he was better than me!
I quickly resolved the feud with payment,
sending treasures to the Wylfings across the sea,
and he swore oaths to me in return.
It pains me to tell anyone
what sorrow Grendel has brought upon me in Heorot,
and the sudden attacks. The hall is empty,

my warriors are dwindling, because fate has taken them
into Grendel's grasp. But God has the power
to vanquish this deadly foe!
Boasting often, as they drank my beer,
the brave men at the ale-cup declared
that they would stand their ground in this banquet hall,
facing Grendel's terror with their blades.
But at morning light, this mead-hall
was drenched in blood, every bench stained,
the hall itself covered in gore. I lost heroes,
brave warriors taken by death.
But now, sit at the feast, speak your words,
brave hero, as your heart desires."
The Geatish men gathered together.
In the grand hall, they took their seats,
strong-willed and determined.
A servant stood by their side,
holding a beautifully crafted cup,
pouring the golden mead.
Musicians played joyous tunes,
filling Heorot with their melodies.
Warriors from the Weder and Dane clans
celebrated together, united and strong.

BOOK VIII

19   Unferth, a son of Ecglaf, spoke out,
       seated at the feet of the leader of the Scyldings.
       He unraveled the stories of Beowulf's feats,
       the brave seafarer, which greatly bothered him.
       He was jealous of those who achieved more
       fame under the heavens in the mortal realm.
       "Are you that Beowulf, the challenger of Breca,
       who swam in the open sea,
       bravely daring the depths
       to test your strength and pride?
       No man, whether willing or unwilling,
       could stop you from your daring swim.
       With your arms, you conquered the ocean tides,
       measured the sea-streets with your strong hands,
       and swam over the waters. Winter's storm
       brought forth rough waves. In the realm of the sea,
       you two struggled for seven nights.
       Though he surpassed you in swimming,
       reaching his destination at dawn,

the waves carried him to the shores of the Battling Reamas,
where he returned to his beloved home,
to the land of the Brondings, a fair fortress,
where he ruled his people and possessed his treasures.
He boasted triumphantly over you, Beowulf.
So I imagine a worse fate for you,
even though you have shown bravery
in the harsh battles and fierce struggles,
if you dare to wait and confront Grendel's approach
through the long night's watch!"
Beowulf, the son of Ecgtheow, answered:
"You have said so much, dear Unferth,
drunk with beer, about the achievements of Breca,
boasting of his victory! But I declare,
that I possessed greater strength in the sea
than any other man, more endurance in the ocean."
We, as young boys full of energy,
boasted and made plans to venture out
into the vast sea, risking our lives.
With naked swords in hand, we swam,
hoping to protect ourselves from whales.
He couldn't drift far away from me,
and I didn't abandon him.
Together, we stayed on the tides
for five whole nights until the waves separated us.
The churning waves, freezing weather,
dark nights, and harsh northern wind
relentlessly attacked us, creating rough surges.
The anger of sea creatures quickly arose.
But thanks to my sturdy and interconnected armor,
made of hard metal links, I received help,
as my breastplate, adorned with gold,
protected me from the monsters.
One hated foe grabbed me tightly

and pulled me down to the depths,
trying to overpower me with a strong grip.
However, I was able to pierce the creature
with the point of my sword,
through the force of my battle blade.
This huge sea beast was defeated
by the tumultuous struggle fought by my hand.

BOOK IX

21 I OFTEN FACED the threat
of these evil monsters. With my sword,
dearly loved, I retaliated against them!
They didn't have the chance to enjoy their plunder
and feast on their victim, those vengeful creatures,
as they lay at the bottom of the sea;
by dawn, they were laid low
by my sword wounds. And since then,
sailors on the boundless sea
are never troubled by them. Then, a bright light
from the east, God's beacon, appeared,
and the waves calmed down
so that I could see the tall cliffs,
wind-swept walls. Fate often saves
a noble warrior if he is brave!
And so it happened that I killed
nine of those water monsters with my sword.
I've never heard of a harder night battle
beneath the sky,

or a more desperate man adrift on the sea!
Yet I emerged unharmed from that hostile grip,
though exhausted from swimming. The sea carried me,
the tide's current, to the shores of Finland,
the rushing waters. I haven't heard
of anyone else who has faced such terrifying swords,
in a bitter battle. Breca, not even you
or anyone else, in the game of war,
has accomplished such a daring feat
with a bloody blade--I don't boast about it!--
even though you were the cause of harm to your dear kin,
your closest relatives. The curse of hell
awaits you, however you may try to use your wit!
Because I say truly, son of Ecglaf,
Grendel would never have committed
such dreadful deeds on your beloved lord,
in Heorot, if your heart
was as courageous as your boastful words!
22　　But he believes there won't be any conflict;
He's confident, thinking he's safe from the fearsome warriors of
your Danish clan.
He disregards the oaths he has made, he doesn't care for the land
of Danes,
He revels in fighting and feasting, not afraid of any feud
with the Spear-Danes. But soon enough
I will prove to him the power and pride of the Geats.
I will challenge him to battle.
Let him have fun now. When the morning light
from the south brings a new day to mankind.
The generous king was overjoyed,
the wise, war-hardened leader. He knew
Beowulf would help, the shepherd of his people.
Laughter filled the hall, as the warriors celebrated,
with joyful words.

Queen Wealhtheow entered,
adorned in gold, showing her graciousness,
greeting the guests.
She first offered the cup
to Hrothgar's heir and protector,
encouraging him to enjoy the feast and drink.
He eagerly took the drink, the renowned king.
Then, Queen Wealhtheow went through the hall,
offering the cup to everyone,
young and old.
Until the moment came,
when the noble-hearted queen approached Beowulf
and presented him with a cup of mead.
She thanked God and praised Beowulf
for granting her hope and providing comfort in times of fear.
Beowulf accepted the cup
with strength and bravery from Queen Wealhtheow's hand.
And eagerly, Beowulf, the son of Ecgtheow, spoke:
"This was my intention when my companions and I
set out on the ocean and boarded our ship,
that I would fulfill the wishes of your people
completely, even if it means facing death
in the clutches of a fiend. I am determined
to perform a courageous deed like any noble warrior,
or meet my end in this very mead-hall."
These words seemed satisfactory to the woman,
Beowulf's bold declaration. The noble lady,
adorned with gold, took her seat next to her husband.
Once again, as before, the warriors began
their merriment and shared words of strength,
celebrating with pride, until finally
King Hrothgar decided it was time to rest for the night.
He understood that a battle awaited them
in the festive hall, once the brightness of the sun faded,

and darkness of night enveloped them,
and shadowy figures began to approach,
pale under the sky. The warriors prepared themselves.
Man to man, Hrothgar addressed Beowulf,
welcoming him and entrusting him with the wine hall:
"Never before have I trusted anyone
to safeguard this noble Danish hall
since I first took up the sword and shield,
but now I bestow this unbeatable house upon you.
Remember your own greatness and show your strength;
be watchful for the enemy! I assure you,
your loyalty will not go unrewarded
if you face the battle with courage and valor."

BOOK X

24 THEN HROTHGAR, surrounded by his warriors,
the protector of the Danes, departed from the hall.
He was eager to seek the company of his queen, proud
Wealhtheow.
The King-of-Glory had assigned a guard
to protect against Grendel, as the heroes heard,
a defender of the hall who watched over the king.
With confidence, the prince of the Geats trusted
in his strength, his power, and the mercy of God!
He took off his iron armor and his helmet,
and gave them to his loyal henchman,
entrusting him to guard his valuable weapons.
Then the brave warrior, Beowulf of the Geats, spoke:
"I do not consider myself weaker in battle,
in fierce war, than Grendel believes himself to be.
But I will not take his life with a sword,
even though I have the power to do so.
He does not possess the skill to strike me,
to cut through my shield, however bold he may be

in battle. Tonight, we both shall reject the sword,
if he dares to attack me unarmed. Let the wise God,
the sacred Lord, decide the outcome
according to His judgment."
Then the leader reclined, with pillows supporting his head,
while the brave seamen sank onto their hall-beds.
None of them knew that their journey from there
to their home and homeland, where they were raised,
would be their last. They knew all too well
that many warriors had met their battle-death
in the banquet-hall of the Danish clan.
But they found comfort and support,
as they weaved their destiny of war, for the people of the Weders.
25 The powerful Master granted the ability,
that one could overpower all their enemies,
with sheer strength alone. It is indeed said
that the supreme God over mankind
has always held this power! In the pale night, walking confidently,
approached the shadowy figure. The warriors slept,
their duty to guard the hall,
except for one. It was widely known
that the ghostly invader could not harm him
against God's will;
alert and prepared, filled with warrior's anger,
he courageously awaited the outcome of the battle.

BOOK XI

 Then from the moorland, by misty crags,
with God's anger loaded, Grendel appeared.
The creature wanted to capture and harm
the people in the magnificent hall.
He walked under the sky until he happily spotted
the hall, which was beautifully decorated.
This was not the first time he sought Hrothgar's home,
but never before had he come across such brave warriors!
The monster approached the house swiftly,
interrupting the peace as he struck down the door.
With great rage, he burst into the house,
breaking through the securely fastened bolts.
He quickly stepped over the beautifully paved floor,
full of anger, with terrifying flashes streaming from his eyes.
He spotted the group of sleeping heroes,
family and loyal followers peacefully gathered.
His heart filled with laughter,
for the monster planned to take their lives in the morning,
as they unsuspectingly awaited a joyous feast.

But fate prevented him from claiming more lives
on that fateful night. Hygelac's relative watched eagerly,
curious about the outcome of this fierce attack.
Not that the monster had any intention of stopping!
Without delay, he seized a slumbering warrior,
tearing him apart with great force,
biting through his bones, and drinking his blood.
Piece by piece, he devoured the lifeless body,
even consuming the feet and hands. Then he proceeded onward.
for the courageous hero, he grabbed with his hand,
felt the foe with his wicked claw,
for the hero who was lying down boldly seized it,
ready to respond, propped on his arm.
Then the shepherd of evil soon realized
that he had never encountered in this world.
Another creature
with a stronger grip put fear in his heart,
and sorrowed in his soul - he couldn't escape so easily!
He wanted to flee, to seek his lair,
the den of demons: he couldn't do
what he had done so many times before!
Then the brave warrior, a loyal follower of Hygelac,
thought about his boast in the evening. He leapt up,
firmly grabbed his foe, whose fingers cracked.
The monster tried to escape, but the warrior pursued closely.
The monster intended--if possible at all--
to free himself and flee far away
to the swamps, for he knew how strong
the grip of his fierce opponent was. This harmful creature
had taken a gruesome march to Heorot!
The room was filled with noise. The Danes lost
their castle and their clan members,
nobles, lost their ale. Both of them were angry,
those savage guards of the hall: the house echoed.

It was a wonder that the wine hall stood strong
in the strain of their struggle, that the beautiful house
did not fall to the ground; it was held tightly
within and without by skillfully placed iron bands;
though many a mead-bench crashed from the windowsill -
they tell me - adorned with gold, where the fierce enemies
wrestled.
The wisest Scyldings had believed
that no man could ever break apart that brave, bone-decorated
house,
destroyed through clever tactics, unless a fiery embrace
enveloped it in smoke. The noise intensified once more.
The people of the North, the Danes,
were filled with fear and panic, every single one,
who heard the wailing from the wall,
the enemy of God singing his dreadful song,
the cry of the defeated, the loud agony
from a captive of hell. He held him too tightly,
the strongest among men
on that very day of our existence.

BOOK XII

29   The earls' defender, the warrior,
refused to let the murderous stranger live,
thinking his life was useless to people on earth.
Many of Beowulf's warriors drew their ancestral swords,
ready to protect their lord's life, their admired prince,
if they could. They didn't know, as they approached the enemy,
these brave war heroes, swinging their swords from all sides
to kill the cursed one, that no sword,
no matter how sharp or well-made,
could hurt that terrible fiend!
Protected by magic, he was immune to swords.
But his end and departure from this life
was destined to be tragic that day,
and his soul would soon go to the demons' realm.
The one who had been cruel and hated by God,
who had killed many, now found his body failing.
Beowulf, Hygelac's determined relative,
held him in his grip; they were enemies to each other.
The outlaw took a fatal wound;

a great gash appeared on his shoulder, sinews snapped,
and bones broke. Beowulf had won the glory,
and Grendel, mortally wounded, went to his den
in the dark moor, a dreadful place.
He knew his life was ending, his time on earth was over.
By this bloody fight, Beowulf had given a gift
to all the Danes. He saved Hrothgar's hall
from destruction. The brave and wise man
had cleansed it again. He was pleased with his night's work,
his bold action. The Danes were happy again,
regaining their old joy. But the earls' defender,
the leader's pride, would be mourned by many
in the future, in sad crowds,
when he was carried to his final resting place.
Such a great earl had never been seen before!
He proved his boast to the people of the East,
the courageous Geat fulfilled his promise,
easing their sorrows and troubles,
carrying the burden of their long-lasting battle,
and the pain they had endured for so long.
The proof was laid bare,
when the brave warrior, with his strong hand,
put an end to Grendel's grip
on their home, under the roof.

BOOK XIII

31   MANY IN THE MORNING, as people have told me,
warriors gathered in the great hall,
leaders from near and far,
traveling far and wide to witness the wonder,
evidence of the traitor. The end of the enemy
didn't trouble anyone
who saw what the enemy had done.
The weary-hearted wretch,
defeated in battle and banished,
had dragged his steps towards death,
marked for doom, towards the devils' lake.
The waves there were bloody and boiling,
the tides tumultuous and turbid,
seething horribly with hot blood from swords,
dyed by the doomed one, in the den of the moor,
he laid down his forlorn life,
his heathen soul, received by hell.
Then the aged warriors rode home,
from that joyful journey,

many young men, on their white horses,
hardy warriors, returned from the lake.
They eagerly praised Beowulf's glory,
and all agreed
that from coast to coast, in any direction,
no other warrior in the land
under the sky's vault, was found to be more brave,
no warrior more worthy of ruling!
(They did not underestimate
their beloved lord, gracious Hrothgar, a good king!)
From time to time, the battle-hardened warriors,
urged on their gray horses to gallop swiftly,
and raced when the road appeared clear.
From time to time, a noble of the king,
who had made many boasts and cherished verses,
familiar with sagas and ancient songs,
recited his well-crafted poems,
weaving his words together in skillful rhyme.
He sang of Beowulf's noble quest,
and cleverly added an excellent tale.
In words well arranged, of the brave acts
he had heard in the saga of Sigemund.
A strange story: he told it all,
the wanderings and struggles of the Waelsing,
which were never told to tribes of men,
the feuds and trickeries, except to Fitela alone,
when he chose to share these stories,
uncle to nephew; always the two
stood side by side in the stress of war,
and together they felled many
monstrous creatures with their swords. Sigemund gained
great praise when he passed away.
The fearless fighter slew a dragon
that guarded a hoard: under an ancient rock

the brave prince dared this dangerous deed
alone on a fearful quest, without Fitela by his side.
But it happened that his sword pierced
the wondrous worm--it struck the wall,
a mighty blow; the dragon died in a pool of blood.
Thus, the fearsome one grasped
control over the treasure hoard,
for his own pleasure. He loaded a ship,
carrying the shining gold
as the son of Waels. The snake was defeated.
He gained the highest reputation
among all the races of men, this protector of warriors,
for his daring deeds that adorned his name
since the hand and heart of Heremod
grew weak in battle. He was swiftly banished,
forced to mingle with monsters, at the mercy of enemies,
betrayed to death. Sorrow overwhelmed him,
a sadness that weighed upon the nobles and princes.
Often, in earlier days,
wise men mourned for the warrior's travels,
hoping for his help in times of danger and distress.
And they had hoped their leader's son would prosper,
follow in his father's footsteps, protect his people,
the treasure, and the fortress, the land of the heroes,
the homeland of the Scyldings. But, according to the thanes,
the kinsman of Hygelac appeared kinder to all,
while the other was provoked by evil deeds!
And once again, they raced along the familiar roads,
covering the ground with the speed of their horses!
The morning sun continued its ascent,
as the brave clansmen hurried
towards the grand hall, eager to witness the spectacle.
The king himself, adorned with glory, the guardian of the
treasure,

led a majestic procession from the bridal chamber.

Alongside him were the queen and her loyal entourage of maidens,

making their way towards the splendid mead-house.

BOOK XIV

34 HROTHGAR SPOKE as he entered the hall,
stood near the steps and gazed at the grand roof,
decorated with gold and marked with Grendel's hand:
"I must swiftly thank the Almighty Ruler
for the sight before me. I have endured
countless sorrows caused by Grendel, but God
continues to perform miracles, the Guardian of Glory.
Until now, I never expected to live long enough
to witness this majestic house, stained with the blood
of the slain and a source of widespread sorrow
to wise men who could not prevent
infernal foes and demonic spirits
from wreaking havoc in this hall. But now,
through the power of the Creator, this hero
has accomplished a feat that none of us
could achieve through cunning or wisdom. Surely,
if the woman who bore this warrior among men
still lives, she can proudly say
that the God of all ages was kind to her

during the birth of her child. Beowulf, from now on,
I love you like a son, the greatest of heroes.
Maintain this newfound kinship, and never
shall you lack the worldly wealth
that I possess. Many a time, I have given
my precious treasure to men of lesser valor
and weaker in battle. But now, with the deeds you have done,
your fame will endure throughout eternity.
May the Creator continue to reward you
as He always has done."
Beowulf, son of Ecgtheow, replied:
"We willingly fought this war,
fearlessly confronting the enemy.
I wish you had witnessed it yourself, the time when"
the evil creature stumbled in his garments, almost falling!
Swiftly, I envisioned, with a strong grip
to bind him down on his death bed,
so he could take his last breath in the hold of my hand:
but he managed to break free.
I could not--it was not the Creator's will--
prevent his escape, although I held
the life-destroyer with a firm grip:
he was too strong, the merciless one, in his fleeing!
However, in his escape, he left behind his hand
as a pledge, his arm and shoulder;
yet, the cursed one could not find any help
through this sacrifice.
He no longer lives, the loathsome fiend,
sunk in his sins. Instead, sorrow holds him,
firmly grasped in the grip of agony,
bound in harmful chains, where he must stay,
an evil outlaw, enduring the dreadful punishment
that the Mighty Creator will impose upon him."
The son of Ecglaf became more silent

about boasting of his battle achievements,
since all noble warriors, witnessing the hand,
gazed at it on the high roof,
the enemy's fingers--the front portion of each
of the sturdy nails resembling steel--
a heathen's "hand-spear," a strange claw
of a hostile warrior. They all agreed,
that no brave blade could touch him,
no matter how sharp, or sever
that battle-stained hand from the sinister foe.

BOOK XV

36 THERE WAS a rush and urgency in Heorot now,
to adorn the hall with hands, and the crowd was thick
with men and women, cleaning the wine-hall,
decorating the guest-room. The hangings gleamed with gold,
woven on the walls, many wonders
to delight all who gazed upon them.
Though the building was reinforced with iron bands,
that bright structure was greatly damaged;
its hinges were torn; only the roof
remained intact, when, consumed by wickedness,
the fiendish foe attempted to flee,
desperate for his life. It is not an easy thing,
finding a way to safety for whoever attempts it!
Driven by fate, he shall discover his path
to the haven prepared for mankind,
for possessors of souls and sons of earth;
and there his body shall rest
after his revelries.
The time had come

for Healfdene's son to enter the hall:
the king himself would sit and feast.
I have never heard of a more noble gathering
assembled around the generous giver of rings!
The bearers of glory bowed to the benches,
eager for the feast. The mighty-in-spirit
received many a mead-cup,
kinsmen who sat in the splendid hall,
Hrothgar and Hrothulf. Heorot now
was filled with friends; the people of Scyldings
had never experienced such treachery.
To Beowulf, the son of Healfdene, gave
a gold-woven banner as a reward for his triumph,
an embroidered battle-flag, a breastplate and helmet;
and many witnessed a splendid sword
being presented to the brave warrior. Beowulf
raised his cup in the hall, filled with gratitude for such valuable gifts.

37 He had no reason to feel ashamed among those brave warriors.
Because I had rarely heard of any heroes, in such a cheerful spirit,
giving such four gifts, so skillfully crafted with gold,
to honor others in such a way!
The helmet had a high ridge on the roof,
wound with wires, protecting the head,
so that no enemy, with sharp weapons,
could harm the hero shielded beneath.
Then, the protector of the earls ordered
eight horses with beautifully adorned bridles
to be led into the hall. One horse
was decorated with a shining saddle and precious jewels;
it was the battle seat fit for the great king,
when the son of Healfdene desired to engage in sword play.
His courage never wavered
in the midst of battle as bodies dropped.

Both the war-steeds and weapons were given
to Beowulf by the king, ruler of the Ingwins,
granting him the right and power over them,
wishing him joy. Honorably,
the mighty prince, guardian of treasures for heroes,
thus repaid his hard-fought battle
with valuable steeds and treasures that no one
can deny are rightfully deserved.

BOOK XVI

38 AND THE NOBLE leader bestowed upon each warrior
who had journeyed with Beowulf across the vast sea
a treasured gift at the feasting table.
They were rewarded with gold,
compensating them for the loss of their comrades,
slain by the monstrous Grendel.
Only the wisest God intervened,
halting the bloodshed and protecting the valiant warriors.
Divine providence guided their destinies,
as it does for all of humanity.
This serves as a reminder
that wisdom and foresight are invaluable,
especially for those who endure the hardships
and conflicts of this world.
Amidst the festivities, the hall resounded
with the harmonious blend of song and music.
Hrothgar, the renowned leader,
listened as the skilled bard recounted the tale
of King Finn's sudden attack on Hnaef and his warriors.

The valiant Scylding, Hnaef,
was destined to fall in the Frisian slaughter.
Hildeburh, a grief-stricken woman,
lost both her beloved son and brother
in the tragic battle.
She mourned their tragic fate
as she beheld their lifeless bodies
lying under the open sky.
The bittersweet beauty of life
had turned into a nightmare.
Finn's own loyal followers were also slain,
leaving only a handful of survivors.
Unable to engage in further conflict,
Finn proposed a truce,
offering peace to Hengest,
the noble warrior serving under Hrothgar.
He hoped to secure the safety
of the remaining members of his retinue
by surrendering his own arms
and acknowledging Hengest's rightful authority.
39 another home the Danes would receive,
a hall and high-seat, and half the authority
to be theirs in Frisian lands;
and for the tribute, Folcwald's son
would daily honor the Danes,
bestowing rings on Hengest's people,
with treasure and jewels,
with intricate goldwork, just as he intended
to honor his Frisian kin in the ale-house.
Further, a firm peace pact was made
by both sides. Finn swore to Hengest
an open oath, promising with honor
to govern the sorrowful remnants,
with the help of wise men,

so that none of the guests
would go against the treaty with words or actions,
or complain with ill intentions
about serving the slayer of their lord,
as men without a leader, as their fate intended.
However, if a Frisian should taunt
the enemy with murderous hatred,
then the sword's edge would seal his fate.
Oaths were given, and ancient gold
was piled from the hoard. The brave warrior
of the Scyldings, the best of battle-thanes,
was laid on his funeral pyre.
Clearly seen in the fire
was the bloody shirt, the gilded boar-crest,
the iron boar, and many nobles
slain by the sword: they fell in battle.
At Hnaef's own pyre, Hildeburh's orders were given,
to place her child's remains upon the flames,
to burn his bones on the funeral pyre,
by his uncle's side. The woman wept
in sorrowful dirges; loud wailing rose.
Then the most intense of funeral pyres
rose to the sky, roaring over the hillock:
heads melted, wounds burst open,
and blood gushed out.
From the wounds on their bodies, the raging fire consumed
the souls of those who were not spared by the violence of war,
from both sides: their strength and liveliness were put out.

BOOK XVII

41   THEN THE BRAVE heroes hurried to see their homeland,
      Alone, they sought the Frisian land,
      With houses and tall fortresses. Hengest
      Still stayed with Finn throughout the death-filled winter,
      Maintaining their peace, but longing for home,
      Although his ship was unable to sail
      Across the restless waves, whipped by fierce winds,
      Or locked in icy chains during winter's grasp.
      Another year passed in the dwellings of men,
      As the sunlit skies faithfully awaited their season.
      Winter was driven far away, leaving the earth peaceful;
      The guest, the wanderer, was eager to depart,
      Although he contemplated seeking vengeance
      More than roaming the vast sea,
      And eagerly awaited the fierce battle
      Where the sons of the Frisians were sure to be.
      Sadly, he did not escape the common fate,
      When Hun with his mighty blade "Lafing"
      Pierced his heart, renowned among Frisian warriors.

Finn, with a wavering spirit, also met his end,
At the hands of Guthlaf and Oslaf, fierce attackers,
Who mourned their own sorrows after landing from the sea.
Finn's uncertain courage could no longer reside in his heart.
The fortress was stained with the blood of enemies,
And Finn, the king among his clansmen, was slain,
While the queen was taken captive.
The Scylding warriors transported all the treasures
They found within Finn's domain, including gems and jewels,
And they led the kind-hearted wife
Across the deep sea to her own land.
The lay came to an end.
At the feast, the minstrel's song filled the air,
and joy spread among the gathered crowd.
The atmosphere brightened as the servants poured
wine from their special vats. Wealhtheow, adorned with a gold
crown,
approached where the king and his nephew sat together,
showing their close bond and mutual loyalty.
Unferth, known for his eloquence, sat at the Scylding lord's feet.
People trusted his spirit and courage,
even though he wasn't the best at sword-fighting.
The Scylding queen, Wealhtheow, spoke up:
"Drink from this cup, my king and lord,
generous giver of gold. Be happy,
and speak kindly to the Geats here.
Enjoy your time with your people. Remember
the gifts you have received, whether they're from near or far.
People tell me you want to adopt
this hero as your son. Enjoy Heorot,
this beautiful jewel-hall, as long as you can,
with many generous gifts. And when it's time
for you to leave, pass your kingdom
to your kin. I trust my Hrothulf

to rule wisely and well, to take care
of our young people if you go first,
prince of the Scyldings. I believe he will repay
our children fairly for everything we've done
to help him gain honor in his early years."
Then she went to where her sons sat,
Hrethric and Hrothmund, surrounded by young warriors.
Beowulf, the brave Geat, was also sitting there,
between the two brothers.

BOOK XVIII

43   A CUP she presented to him, with a friendly greeting
    and kind words. Made of gold, finely crafted,
    she offered him two arm bracelets, a shining corselet,
    rings, and the most noble collars
    that I have ever seen on this earth.
    Never before have I heard of such a magnificent treasure,
    a gem of heroes under the heavens,
    since Hama took the Brisings' necklace
    to his splendid city, a jewel and gem-filled chest.
    He chose eternal aid, leaving behind Eormenric's hatred.
    Hygelac, the Geat, Swerting's grandson,
    carried this ring with him on his last journey,
    defending his spoils under his banner,
    guarding his war treasures. But fate overwhelmed him
    when, in his bravery, he sought danger
    and feuded with the Frisians. The most beautiful of gems
    he carried with him across the ocean waves,
    mighty and regal. He died under his shield.
    The Franks obtained the king's body,

the treasure of his chest, and that glorious ring.
Weaker warriors seized the spoils,
after fierce battles, from the lord of the Geats,
and claimed the field of death.
The noise grew in the hall.
Wealhtheow, speaking among the warriors, said:
"Enjoy this jewel in your joyful youth,
beloved Beowulf, wear this armor in battle,
a royal treasure, and prosper greatly!
Preserve your strength and be kind to these young men,
let gratitude be my reward.
You have achieved such greatness
that you are celebrated for many days to come,
as far and wide as the ocean waves reach
with their windy shores. May you thrive
and possess riches throughout your life. I pray for you,
O prince! And for my son, may he find joy and peace."
be helpful, make him happy!
Here, every nobleman is loyal to each other,
kind-hearted and faithful to their lord!
The thanes are friendly, the group is obedient,
loyal subjects reveling: listen and obey!"
She then went back to her seat. That was the grandest of feasts;
wine flowed for the warriors. They were unaware of fate,
the dreadful destiny that many a nobleman would witness
when evening came and Hrothgar would return home,
weary but regal, to rest. The room was protected
by an army of noble warriors, just as before.
They removed the benches; they placed
beds and pillows. One heavy drinker
in danger of doom lay down in the hall.
They placed their shields of war above their heads,
bright bucklers. On the bench,
every nobleman had

a shining battle-helmet, a proud spear,
and a chain shirt. It was their custom
to always be prepared for battle,
whether at home or at battle
whenever their brave king faced
danger. They were loyal.

BOOK XIX

45 THEN THEY FELL ASLEEP. One person with sadness
     bought their evening rest, as had often happened
     when Grendel guarded that beautiful hall,
     causing evil until his end drew near,
     punishment for his sins. It was seen and told
     how a champion avenged against the fiend,
     as was learned from far away. For a long time
     after that fierce battle, Grendel's mother,
     a monstrous woman, mourned her loss.
     She was condemned to dwell in the cold waters,
     in the depths of the sea, since Cain killed
     his own brother with a sword,
     becoming an outlaw, marked with the crime,
     banished from the joys of humanity,
     and wandering the wilderness. From him
     rose such fate-bound monsters as Grendel,
     a horrific war-wolf, who came upon
     a warrior watching and awaiting the fight at Heorot,
     and with whom the gruesome one grappled fiercely.

But the man remembered his great strength,
the glorious gift that God had given him,
and in God's mercy, he placed his trust
for comfort and help. So he conquered the enemy,
defeated the fiend, who fled in disgrace,
deprived of joy, to the realm of death,
the enemy of mankind. And now his mother,
dark and grim, sought to avenge her son's death.
She came to Heorot, where the helmeted Danes
slept in the hall. But the old troubles returned
when she burst in,
Grendel's mother. Yet, this terror was less grim,
less fearful than the terror of a woman in war,
the strength of a maiden compared to armed men,
when a forged hammer strikes a hard sword,
a sword that is stained with gore, cutting through the helmet's tusks.

46   Swords clashed, cutting through the air,
As the harsh blades were drawn in the hall.
Many sat on benches, gripping shields firmly in hand,
Neglecting their helmets and armor,
Frightened by the horror that overtook them.
Swiftly, she fled, desperate to escape
The watchful eyes of the loyal warriors.
Yet, she managed to seize one young nobleman,
Holding onto him tightly as she made her way to the moor.
He was Hrothgar's most cherished and trusted person,
Known among the seas.
She killed him on his own bed, a brave warrior in battle.
But Beowulf was not there.
He had been given a separate house
After receiving his share of gold, as the renowned Geat.
Heorot was filled with chaos as everyone witnessed
The blood-stained evidence she carried with her.

Sorrow filled the dwellings, a dreadful exchange,
Where both Danes and Geats were forced to sacrifice
The lives of their loved ones.
The aged king, the tested ruler,
Felt a deep sadness in his heart
When he realized his noble warrior was no longer alive,
And that his dearest thane was truly dead.
Beowulf was quickly brought to his presence,
Victorious and fearless. As dawn broke,
He entered the hall with his loyal men,
Seeking the wise old king, lord of the Ingwines,
And inquired about the prince's peaceful night.

BOOK XX

47   Hrothgar, the leader of the Scyldings, spoke:
      "Do not ask about joy! Sorrow has returned
      to the Danish people. Aeschere is dead,
      the elder brother of Yrmenlaf,
      my wise advisor and support in meetings,
      a companion in battle when warriors clashed,
      in defense of our heads, we fought,
      slashing at helmets. Every noble should mourn
      the loss of Aeschere, a renowned hero!
      But here in Heorot, a supernatural being
      has killed him. I do not know where
      the proud creature, hungry for flesh,
      went after claiming her victim.
      Last night, she sought revenge,
      unyielding, for the feud, mercilessly,
      after you, with fierce strength, killed Grendel,
      who had been destroying and ravaging
      my loyal warriors for far too long.
      He fell in battle, deprived of life.

Now, another creature comes,
ruthless and vengeful, seeking to avenge her kin,
traveling far in a blood feud,
causing many warriors to believe, whoever
grieves for that ring-giver, that this is the most painful
of all heartaches. The one who was once willing
to grant every wish lies lifeless.
The people who live in this land,
neighbors of mine, have told me
that they have sometimes encountered such a pair,
enormous wanderers haunting the moors,
restless spirits: one of them appeared,
as far as my people could tell,
to be a woman, and the other, accursed,
walked the path of misery in the guise of a man,
though larger than any human.
Long ago, the people of this land named him Grendel,
but they don't know who his father was
or any offspring he might have had,
born from treacherous spirits. Their dwelling is uncharted;
They linger near cliffs where wolves roam,
on windy headlands and fearful fenways,
where a stream flows from mountain to rocky gloom,
an underground river. It is not far from here,
in terms of miles, that the lake expands,
covered by a frost-bound forest,
with sturdy roots casting shadows on the water.
At night, a strange wonder can be seen,
fire on the waters. No wise man
among the sons of men dared to explore those depths!
Even if a hunted deer, pursued by dogs,
were to seek refuge in this forest,
after a long chase, it would rather surrender
its dear life on the shore than plunge into the unknown

to hide its head. It is not a happy place!
From there, the turmoil of waves washes up,
pale against the sky when winds stir
evil storms, and the air grows dark,
and the heavens weep. Now, once again,
you alone can provide help! The land is unfamiliar to you,
a place of fear, where you will discover
that sinful being. Go, if you dare!
I will reward you, for engaging in this battle,
with ancient treasure, just as I did before,
with winding gold, if you succeed in returning it."

BOOK XXI

49 Beowulf spoke with wisdom, son of Ecgtheow:
"Do not grieve, wise one! It is better for us
to seek revenge for our friends than to mourn them in vain.
All of us must face our end
in this world's ways. Let those who can
win glory before death! The most honorable fate
for a warrior is to die a courageous death.
Rise, protector of the kingdom! Let us ride at once,
and follow the trail of Grendel's mother.
No hiding place shall shield her - take my word! -
whether it be fields or forested mountains,
or the depths of the sea, she shall not escape!
But for now, endure patiently,
as I believe you will, each of your hardships."
The elder warrior leaped up, giving thanks to God,
the mighty Lord, for the man's brave words.
A horse was quickly saddled for Hrothgar,
a majestic and strong steed. The wise king
rode with dignity, his men armed with shields

followed close behind. The footprints led
through the woods, easily seen,
a path across the plains, where she had passed
and walked upon the dark moor. She carried
the lifeless body of the bravest and noblest warrior,
one who ruled the kingdom with Hrothgar.
Onward, then, the prince-born hero continued
crossing steep cliffs and narrow passages,
unfamiliar ways, sheer cliffs, and the dwellings of the water-
monsters.
He led the way, with a few wise men by his side
to navigate the paths until he suddenly found
a forested hill overlooking a gray rock,
a mournful forest where the waves below
were stained with blood. The Danish warriors
felt great sorrow, and for all the Scyldings,
for many heroes, it was difficult to bear.
Sad for the noble warriors, when they found
Aeschere's head by the river, on the shore.
The waves were churning, the warriors saw,
red with blood; the horn sang its battle-song
loudly and bravely. The group sat down,
and watched strange, serpent-like creatures
in the water--sea dragons that filled the deep,
and dangerous monsters resting on the shore--
they often embark on their ruthless quest
at the break of dawn, searching for ships to attack--
sea snakes and beasts. These creatures, alarmed,
swam away, disturbed by the sound
of the war-horn. The Geatish leader
shot a swift arrow from his bow,
striking down one of the terrifying monsters,
piercing its heart; in the water, it appeared
less mighty in swimming, now that death had seized it.

Swiftly, with well-hooks and barbed boar-spears,
they attacked the struggling creature,
killing it and dragging it to the shore,
a wondrous sea-roamer. The warriors looked in awe
at the fearsome sight.
Then Beowulf adorned himself
in sturdy armor, without fear for his life.
His broad, bright breastplate, hand-woven,
would withstand the test of the waters.
It would protect his body from the blows of battle,
shielding his heart from the hands of his enemies.
And his white helmet, that covered his head,
was prepared to face the depths of the flood,
to conquer the swirling waves. It was adorned with chains,
decorated with gold, just as in ancient times
a skilled weapon-smith crafted it,
setting it with images of boars, so that no sword could harm it.
Nor was that the least of the powerful aids
that Hrothgar's spokesman gave in their time of need:
"Hrunting" they called the sword with hilt,
a treasure from ancient times, the finest of its kind;
its iron edge was etched with venom,
hardened with battle-blood, unwavering in combat
in the hand of a hero who wielded it,
ready to face perilous paths
towards the enemies' dwellings. This sword
had been destined long ago to perform such daring tasks.
For the son of Ecglaf, strong and sturdy,
did not remember the boast he had made,
when he was drunk with wine, as he lent this weapon
to a more courageous warrior. But he himself
dared not risk his life
under the churning waters as a loyal retainer.

Thus, he lost his fame,
the respect of noble men. But the other,
who now girded himself for the grim battle, did not.

BOOK XXII

52 Beowulf spoke, son of Ecgtheow:

"Remember, esteemed descendant of Healfdene,
friend of men, as I embark on this quest,
wise king, remember what was once said:
if I were to lose my life in your cause,
you would remain loyal to me, even in death,
taking my father's place!
Be a protector to my group of warriors,
my friends in battle, if War should seize me,
and send the noble gifts you bestowed upon me,
beloved Hrothgar, to Hygelac!
Let the king of Geatland see through the gold,
let Hrethel's son behold, as he gazes upon the treasure,
that I have gained a friend renowned for his goodness,
and that I rejoiced while I could in my generous benefactor.
And let Unferth wield this extraordinary sword,
esteemed nobleman, this precious heirloom,
sharp and deadly: with Hrunting, I
seek glory or accept death."

After speaking these words, the lord of the Weder-Geats
boldly hastened, with no intentions to wait
for any reply: the ocean waves
swallowed the hero. It took a long time
before he felt the sea floor beneath his feet.
Soon, the monster who ruled the underwater domain
for centuries, hungry for bloodshed,
realized that a guest from above,
a man, was invading her territory.
She reached out for him with her gruesome claws,
and the warrior grabbed hold of her;
but she didn't harm his healthy body,
his breastplate protected him
as she tried to break through his war-shirt,
the linked armor, with her repulsive hand.
Then, when she reached the ocean floor,
this sea-wolf carried the lord of rings to her lair she inhabited.
While bravely he fought, his courage unwavering,
struggling against monstrous creatures
that fiercely attacked him; many sea beasts
tried to tear his armor with sharp tusks,
swarming around the stranger. But soon he realized
he was now in some hall, though he didn't know which,
where water could never harm him,
and the roof above protected him
from the jaws of the flood. He saw the light of a fire,
beams of a blazing fire that shone brightly.
Then the warrior saw that deep-water creature,
a monstrous merewife. With a mighty swing
of his blade, he struck without hesitation.
The blade sang its wild battle-song upon her head.
But the warrior discovered
that the blade, meant for fighting,
did not bite, did not harm the creature's heart.

Its sharp edge failed the noble warrior,
even though it had known in the past
the strife of hand-to-hand combat, and had shattered helmets
and the gear of doomed men. It was the first time
that this gleaming blade had failed in its glory.
Still, the warrior stood firm, his valor unwavering,
mindful of great deeds, a kinsman of Hygelac;
he discarded the ornate sword, adorned with jewels,
in his anger; it lay on the ground,
sharp-edged and stiff. He trusted instead
in his own strength, the grip of his mighty hand.
That's what a man must do
when he seeks to earn lasting fame in battle,
without fear for his own life!
Weary from the fight, the warrior stumbled,
the fiercest of fighters, he fell to the ground.
The hall guest pounced on him, wielding her short sword,
wide and sharp, seeking revenge for her lost child,
the only son. On his shoulder, he wore
a strong coat of mail, protecting him from death,
shielding him from the edge of the blade.
Ecgtheow's son would have surely perished,
buried deep beneath the earth, this brave Geat,
if his sturdy armor hadn't saved him,
his hard battle gear, and if the wise Creator,
the holy God, hadn't determined his victory.
The Lord of Heaven was on his side,
and the brave warrior easily stood up again.

BOOK XXIII

55 Amidst the armor, he spotted a victorious sword,
an ancient weapon of the giants, with a blade of strength,
a prized possession of warriors, a weapon unmatched,
which only the strongest could wield in battle –
crafted by giants, sharp and ready.
The leader of the Scyldings then seized its chain-hilt,
bold and fierce in battle, he brandished the sword,
fearless of his own life, and struck with great fury
until it gripped her neck and held her tight,
breaking her bone-rings as the blade pierced through
the doomed one's flesh, causing her to collapse on the floor.
The blade was covered in blood, but he felt joyous for his deed.
Then a bright light illuminated the hall,
as if an unclouded candle from the sky was shining.
He surveyed the hall and moved towards the wall,
raising his weapon high by the hilt,
filled with anger and eagerness, the loyal warrior.
This blade was not useless to him now.
He wanted to reward Grendel swiftly for his fierce attacks,

for the wars he waged on the people of the Western-Danes,
more than just one time,
when he killed Hrothgar's companions as they slept,
devouring them mercilessly,
fifteen men from the tribe of Danes,
and taking away just as many more,
his horrendous prize. The vengeful prince
was well compensated for that.
For now he saw Grendel lying there, defeated in battle,
devoid of life, left maimed by the battle in Heorot.
The body flew far when the fatal blow,
the savage sword-strike, severed its head.
Soon, the wise companions witnessed this scene.
In Hrothgar's company, the waiting men
observed the turbulent waves grow murky,
the mere stained with blood. A group of aged men,
grey-haired and wise, spoke of the warrior
who they believed would not return,
proud from his triumph, to seek
their esteemed leader. It seemed to many
that the wolf of the waves had claimed his life.
As the ninth hour approached, the noble Scyldings
left the headland and made their way home,
leaving the guests behind, gazing at the surging waters,
filled with sorrow and longing, but uncertain
if they would see their beloved lord again.
Then, something extraordinary occurred:
the sword, drenched in battle's blood,
began to diminish, melting away like ice
when the Father of Frost loosens its grip,
unraveling the bonds of winter. It was the work
of the true God, controlling all seasons and times.
The Geatish prince took nothing from that dwelling
except the monster's head and the jewel-adorned hilt.

The blade had melted, consumed by the heat
of the demon's poisonous blood, the fiend who perished within.
Soon, the victorious warrior emerged from the waters,
having witnessed the downfall of the demons,
resurfacing through the flood. The clash of the waves
had now subsided, no longer a treacherous expanse,
as the wicked creature ended her days
in this world of fleeting existence.
With strength and resolve, he swam to the shore,
grateful for his salvation, carrying with him
a brave burden of sea-booty.
His loyal band of warriors greeted him warmly,
thanking God for their chieftain's safe return,
They rejoiced to see him safe and sound once more.
Soon, the courageous warrior removed his helmet and armor
skillfully. Now, the calm waters of the lake
were stained with the blood of battle.
They journeyed forth along familiar paths,
with joyful hearts, measuring the well-known roads.
Valiant men carried Grendel's decapitated head
from the cliff by the sea, a difficult task
that required the strength of four men
to bear it to the golden hall.
And so, they arrived at the palace,
fearless enemies, fourteen Geats,
marching together. Among them, their leader,
mighty and revered, strode proudly.
Then, the brave and renowned Hrothgar
entered the hall without fear,
greeting his loyal thanes.
And following closely behind, Grendel's head
was brought into the hall, where the warriors were drinking,
a sight that filled the entire clan and the queen with awe,
a wondrous monster for all to behold.

BOOK XXIV

  Beowulf spoke, son of Ecgtheow:
   "Look, we have brought you this treasure from the sea,
   son of Healfdene, lord of the Scyldings.
   It is a symbol of our great victory. Look at it here.
   I did not escape with my life easily!
   I ventured underwater to fight this battle,
   giving endless effort, and even then,
   I would have died if the Lord had not protected me.
   I could not rely on Hrunting
   during this war, although it is a good weapon.
   Instead, the Lord granted me a sword
   that I discovered hanging on the wall,
   old and massive. How often He aids
   the friendless! With that sword, I fought
   the guardians of the evil creature's lair.
   It burned brightly, its blade glowing,
   as the blood of my enemies spilled over it,
   mixing with my hot battle sweat.
   I returned to you with the hilt of that sword,

having avenged the wicked deeds
and the deaths of the Danes.
Now, I promise you this:
you can sleep safely in Heorot,
alongside your soldiers,
both the old and the young.
Do not fear any harm, Lord of the Scyldings,
from that side again,
no ill will come upon your warriors, as it did before!"
Then, they placed the golden hilt in the hands
of the gray-haired leader, the old hero,
a magnificent and ancient creation.
Now, it belonged to the Danish lord,
after the defeat of the demons,
the work of skilled craftsmen,
since the world had been freed
from the monstrous fiend,
who was marked by murder, along with his mother.
And now, it was in the possession of the king of the people.
59 Mightiest of all the kings of the sea
Who have spread their treasures across the land of Scandia.
Hrothgar spoke, his eyes fixed on the ancient hilt,
An heirloom that bore the marks
Of a legendary battle long ago,
When the giants were swallowed by the raging waves,
A cursed race, shunned by the Eternal God.
In those perilous waters, they met their deserved fate,
And the Wielder of the sword paid them their due.
Engraved on the gleaming golden guard
Were ancient runes, prophesying
For whom this serpent-adorned sword was forged,
The finest blade of a bygone age,
With a skillfully wrapped hilt. Wise Hrothgar spoke,
Son of Healfdene, and silence fell upon the crowd:

"Truly, he who follows the path of truth and righteousness,
Guiding his people with ancient wisdom,
Is a guardian of the land, and you, Beowulf,
Belong to the noblest lineage! Thus, let your fame
Spread far and wide, among many lands.
With your mighty strength and wise spirit,
You shall uphold all that is just and true.
I assure you, my dear friend, of my unwavering love,
As I promised before. In the years to come,
You will be a steadfast support
For your people, a beacon of hope. Unlike Heremod,
Who brought only destruction and death
To the descendants of Ecgwela, the honorable Scyldings.
He, driven by anger, slaughtered his own comrades,
His companions at the feast. Alone, he departed,
A proud leader, without human companionship.
Although the Creator bestowed upon him great power,
Delighting in his rule above all others,
His heart was consumed by a thirst for blood,
His treasure in his breast grew, but he gave no bracelets
to the Danes as was expected. He endured the joyless
burden of struggle and the weight of sorrow,
an enduring feud with his own people. Take this as a lesson!
Let virtue guide you! I have spoken this verse for you,
wise from many winters gone by. Remarkable it seems
how Almighty God sends wisdom to the sons of men
through the strength of His spirit,
giving honor and high status. He controls all things.
Sometimes He allows the heart of a noble hero
to prosper mightily,
granting him a joyful seat in his ancestral home,
a sure fortress for his people to rely on,
giving him great power over vast lands,
an expansive kingdom that this seeker of wisdom

believes to have no end.
So he thrives in wealth, unaffected by
illness or old age. There are no worries of evil
to darken his spirit, no swords of enemies threaten
him from any direction. The whole world
obeys his will, and he knows no worse,
until within him, stubborn pride
grows and awakens while the guardian sleeps,
the sentinel of the spirit. His sleep is too deep
to master his strength, and the slayer draws near,
quietly shooting arrows from his bow!

BOOK XXV

61   "UNDERNEATH HIS ARMOR, his heart is struck
    by the sharpest arrows; no shelter can stop
    the wicked desires of the demonic fiend.
    He finds his long-held possessions meager,
    greedy and grim, withholding golden rings
    as a display of his pride. He forgets
    the promised future, rejecting all that God,
    the Creator of wonders, has bestowed upon him--
    wealth and fame. Yet, inevitably,
    the frail body succumbs and falls,
    destined to be succeeded by another
    who gladly divides the jewels,
    the royal riches, without regard for his predecessor.
    Therefore, dear Beowulf, banish such harmful thoughts,
    be the best of men and choose the path
    of eternal gain. Hold back your pride,
    renowned warrior! Your strength may flourish now,
    but soon it will wane,
    be it from sickness or sword, fire or flood,

blade or spear, the weariness of old age,
or the fading of your once bright eyes.
Even you, hero of war, shall be quickly overwhelmed
by Death. For a hundred half-years,
I ruled the Ring-Danes, protecting them bravely
from numerous powerful beings across the earth,
from spears and swords, until it seemed to me
that no enemy could be found beneath the sky.
But behold, a sudden shift! In my secure seat,
joy turned to grief when Grendel began
to terrorize my home, that hellish foe.
For those relentless attacks, I endured
heavy sorrow in my heart. Thanks be to Heaven,
the Eternal Lord, for extending my life."
I gaze at my head, hewn and bloodied,
after enduring long evil.
Go to the bench now! Be happy at the feast,
worthy warrior! A wealth of treasure
will be shared between us at dawn!"
The Geats' lord was glad, going early
to find his seat, as the Sage commanded.
Once again, a splendid banquet was prepared
for the famous warriors in the hall.
The Night-Helm darkened, casting dusk
over the drinkers.
The brave ones rose,
for the aged Scylding desired rest,
and the eager Geat, a sturdy shield-fighter,
longed for sleep.
A weary wanderer from afar,
a hall-thane who customarily cared for the needs
of warriors as in days of old,
heralded the stout-hearted guest.
And so, the guest slumbered.

The hall stood tall and grand,
gabled and adorned, where the guest slept
until a black raven signaled the joyful dawn.
Brightness emerged from the darkness,
and the swordsmen hurried,
eager to journey homeward.
Far from there, the great-hearted guest
would guide his ship.
Then the courageous one asked for Hrunting,
to be brought to the son of Ecglaf.
He took the excellent iron sword,
thanked its owner,
and praised its battle-worthiness,
calling it a "friendly ally in war."
He did not speak ill of its sharpness.
Truly, he was a great-hearted man!
Now, armed and ready to part ways,
the warriors waited as their host went
That beloved leader of the Danes. The brave prince
quickly approached the throne and greeted Hrothgar.

BOOK XXVI

64   Beowulf spoke, son of Ecgtheow:
"Listen, we sailors share our desire,
men from afar, as we eagerly seek
Hygelac now. We have found ourselves
welcome here, you have sheltered us well.
If I am ever able to earn more
of your love, O noble leader,
beyond what I have already done,
I am willing to continue my warrior's work!
If I come across any enemies
from neighboring lands who harm and threaten you,
as those who have hated you before have done,
I will bring thousands of thanes,
brave heroes to help you. I know that Hygelac,
the protector of his people, although he is young,
the lord of the Geats will offer me aid
with words and actions, so that I may serve you well,
using my skills in battle to secure your victory
and lending you strength when you need more men.

If your son Hrethric should come to the court of the Geats,
a prince by birth, he will surely find
friends there. It is wise for every man
who boasts of bravery to visit distant lands."
In response, Hrothgar spoke to him:
"The wisest God has sent these words
to your soul! I have not heard
such wise counsel from someone so young before.
You are strong and cautious in both body and mind,
wise in your words! I truly believe
that if ever Hrethel's heir
is seized by spear, by fierce sword battles,
by illness or iron, and you survive,
the Sea-Geats will find no better man
to choose as their chief and king,
as the protector of heroes, if you agree."
Your kinsman's kingdom, your keen mind pleases me,
more and more, Beowulf, I am fond of you!
You have brought about peace between our people,
the Geats and the Spear-Danes,
putting an end to the murderous conflict,
that once plagued us with war.
As long as I am ruler of this great realm,
let our treasures be shared, let heroes
exchange gold as they greet each other,
let the ships carry signs of love
across the rolling waves. I believe my people
are bound together, both in friendship and in the face of hatred,
and they hold dear the traditions of honor."
In the hall, Healfdene's son then
presented twelve treasures to Beowulf,
as a token of trust and asked him to return
safely to his beloved people.
The renowned king embraced

the choicest of his thanes and wept.
Heavy with the weight of many winters,
he had two chances to see his friend again,
to hear his voice in the hall. Beowulf was so dear to him,
his wild emotions couldn't be restrained;
a secret longing burned in his soul,
locked deep within his mind. Beowulf, then, walked
proudly across the grass, grateful for the gifts.
The ship waited at anchor, eagerly anticipating its owner.
As they continued their journey, they praised
Hrothgar's generous gift for a long while.
He was an unparalleled lord, faultless in every way,
until old age caught up with him.
it harms no person, his great strength.

BOOK XXVII

67   THEY ARRIVED AT THE OCEAN, the always brave
       and tough followers, carrying their armor,
       crafted war-shirts. The watchman noticed,
       as reliable as ever, the earl's return.
       From the hilltop, no hostile words
       reached the guests as he rode to welcome them;
       but "Welcome!" he called to that group from Weder,
       as the shiny-armored warriors marched to the ship.
       Then on the shore, with their horses and treasure
       and armored ship, spacious and adorned with rings,
       they loaded heavily: its mast stood high
       above Hrothgar's precious gems.
       Beowulf gave a sword to the boat-guard,
       inlaid with gold; since he possessed that blade,
       an old heirloom, he was highly esteemed on the mead-bench.
       Boarding their ocean-going ship,
       they sailed through the deep, leaving Daneland.
       A sea-cloth was set, a sail with ropes,
       firmly attached to the mast, the timbers creaked,

nor did the wind blow the wave-swimmer
off course, over the billows. The boat sped on,
its foamy neck floating above the waves,
the keel securely bound by salty currents,
until they caught sight of the familiar cliffs
of Geatish land. The boat, driven by winds,
came up onto the shore.
The helpful harbor-guard stood at the haven,
who had long awaited and watched from afar
for his beloved companions by the water.
He tied the wide-breasted ship to the beach
with anchor ropes, so that the trusty timber
would not be torn away by the ocean's waves.
Then Beowulf instructed them to bring the treasure,
gold and jewels. It wasn't a long journey
from there to the giver of rings.
Hygelac, a noble lord, resided
by the fortified sea-wall, along with his kinsmen.
Proud was his house, with the king a great hero,
the hall tall and spacious, and Hygd, his young queen,
wise and cautious, though she had spent only a few winters
within the fortress walls, as the daughter of Haereth.
She was neither humble in her ways,
nor reluctant to give gifts to the Geatish men,
bestowing precious treasures upon them.
Unlike the infamous Queen Thryth, she did not display
pride or wickedness. No one dared to be so bold
(except her husband alone) as to meet her gaze directly.
Otherwise, they would suffer a fate as dire
as being bound by deathly chains!
Her vengeance would be swift and unforgiving.
It was not fitting for a queen to inflict harm
upon her beloved warriors through wrath and deception!
However, the kinsman of Hemming prevented this.

During their gatherings over ale, men also spoke
about how, after she became a golden-adorned bride
to the brave young prince, Offa,
she toned down her acts of terror,
and instead brought blessings and peace to the people.
She had crossed the distant river, at the command of her father,
to Offa's magnificent hall, where she thrived
as a prosperous queen, blessed with wealth,
content with the good life that fate had granted her,
and loyal in her love for the noble warrior lord.
Of all the heroes I have heard about
from far and wide, across the seas,
Offa was the most remarkable.
He was praised by many for his bravery in battle
and his generosity towards his subjects.
The valiant warrior, Eomer, stood as a wise ruler
over his kingdom. He was Hemming's relative
and descended from Garmund,
a fierce warrior famous in battle.

BOOK XXVIII

70   HE HURRIED, accompanied by his loyal followers,
to walk along the sandy shore and open paths.
The sun, like a great candle, illuminated the world
as it shone from the southern sky. They walked
with determined steps towards the familiar place
where the young king, a slayer of Ongentheow,
resided in his stronghold, a refuge for heroes.
The news of Beowulf's arrival quickly reached
Hygelac in the court, the shelter for his followers,
where his loyal companion returned alive and well
from his heroic exploits. Upon his sovereign's command,
space was made in the hall for the travelers.
Beowulf sat beside his lord, safe from battle,
among his kinsmen. He first greeted his gracious lord
with respectful words. The daughter of Haereth,
a beautiful maiden who served the warriors,
came through the hall carrying a wine-cup
to offer to the heroes. Hygelac then
inquired of his companion in the noble hall,

eager to hear about the adventures of the Sea-Geats.
"What happened during your journey, my kinsman Beowulf,
when your desires suddenly led you across
the sea to seek battle in Heorot?
Were you able to assist Hrothgar,
the respected leader, in his well-known troubles?
My heart was filled with worry, as I strongly questioned
your decision to face that murderous monster.
I had begged you for a long time
not to confront Grendel, but to allow
the South-Danes to resolve their feud
on their own. Now, thank God,
I can see you now, safe and unharmed!"
Beowulf spoke, son of Ecgtheow:
"It is known to many, Lord Hygelac,
about the fierce battle between Grendel and me,
that took place on the battlefield where
he brought much sorrow upon the Scylding people.
I avenged them all.
No one from Grendel's family can boast
about the chaos
caused by the longest-living member
of that loathsome race! But first, I went
to greet Hrothgar in the hall of gifts,
where the famous kinsman of Healfdene
immediately gave me a seat
next to his son and heir, as soon as
he understood my purpose.
The warriors were lively. In all my life
I have never heard such cheerful men
in the hall, drinking mead, under heaven!
The noble queen, the bringer of peace,
passed through the hall, cheering the young warriors
and offering them golden clasps,

before she took her seat and gave presents to others.
Hrothgar's daughter, Freawaru, often
served the ale-cup to the heroes in turn,
as I heard these companions of the hall
call her name. She offered gold
to the warriors. She is promised
to Froda's happy son, a maiden adorned with gold.
The wise Scylding's friend, the protector of the kingdom,
deems it right to wed her and prevent fighting
and bloodshed. But it rarely happens
that the spear that causes deaths
remains still for long, even if the bride is fair!
"And the Lord of the Heathobards will unlikely be pleased,
And like each loyal warrior in the Danes' ranks,
when a nobleman of the Danes walks with the lady
within their grand hall, adorned with heirlooms,
shining and decorated with rings, treasures of the Heathobard,
weapons once proudly wielded
until they were lost at the fateful battle.
A wise elder, pondering over the ale,
recalls the deadly strife of men, stern in demeanor,
burdened in heart, and he tests the young hero,
probing his character and stirring up hatred for war with these words:
"Don't you recognize, my comrade, that sword
which your father carried into battle,
that precious blade, when he was slain by the Danish,
and the war-torn land mourned the fall of Withergild,
after the hero's destruction, the valiant Scyldings?
Now, the son of a merciless Dane,
proud of his spoils, parades in this hall,
delighting in killing, and possessing the jewel
that rightfully belongs to you!"
Thus, he persistently incites him

with sharp words until an opportunity arises,

where Freawaru's loyal warrior, as retribution for his father's deeds,

must fall in bloodshed, succumbing to the bite of a sword,

while that loyal warrior flees to a land he knows.

And thus, the promises of both nobles are broken,

as Ingeld's heart fills with hatred for war,

and his love for his wife wanes after the storms of conflict.

"So, I do not trust the faith of the Heathobards."

because of the Danes, or their love

and peace agreement. But I won't focus on that,

let's turn to Grendel, the one who brought terror,

and let me explain in detail how the fight went,

the battle of heroes. When the precious gem of the sky

had disappeared in the distance, that ferocious spirit came,

a savage enemy of the night, searching for us

where we guarded the hall, safe and sound.

Hondscio was the first to suffer from that terrifying creature,

his fate was to fall. Grendel turned his murderous mouth

towards our mighty kinsman,

devouring the brave man's entire body.

But the bloodthirsty murderer didn't leave the golden hall empty-handed,

for me, he attacked in his fear of my strength,

his greedy hand grabbing me. He had a glove hanging from him,

large and marvelous, adorned with bands,

carefully crafted by devilish skill, made from dragon's skin.

He wanted to thrust me there, an innocent man,

among many others. But he couldn't do it,

when I stood angrily upright.

It would take too long to explain how I avenged

the destruction caused by that land-destroyer;

but because of this, my lord, your people

gained fame through my fighting. He fled,

and for a short time, he managed to preserve his life.
He left his stronger hand behind in Heorot,
that outcast fell, with a heart full of sorrow,
on the ocean floor.
For this battle, the friend of the Scyldings
rewarded me generously with plates of gold,
with many treasures, when morning arrived.
and we all sat down at the banquet table.
Then there was singing and laughter. The old Scylding,
wise and experienced, spoke of times long ago.
As the hero played his harp,
bringing joy to our hearts, he sang
of truth and sadness, or shared
legends of wonder, this noble king;
sometimes longing for his youth,
remembering old battles now in his aging years,
the aged hero whose heart swelled
with the passing of time.
So in the hall, we spent the entire day
feasting and enjoying ourselves, until night fell
over the land. Then, eagerly seeking vengeance,
Grendel's mother appeared, full of sorrow.
Her son was dead, killed by the warriors of the Weders;
now, this monstrous woman, filled with rage, sought to
avenge her offspring. She killed Aeschere, a loyal
counselor of King Hrothgar, and when morning came,
the Danes could not even lay their fallen comrade
on a funeral pyre to be burned.
She had carried the corpse to her underwater lair
with cruel hands. This was the greatest sorrow
for Hrothgar, burdening the lord of his people.
Then, the leader, desperate and sorrowful,
begged me with his life at stake,
to be the hero and risk my own life

for the sake of glory and honor. He promised me a reward.
So I went to the waters – as the story goes –
and there I found that savage guardian of the sea floor.
We fought hand to hand for a while;
the waves filled with blood in that briny hall.
I swung my brave sword and severed the head
of Grendel's mother, saving my own life,
though not without facing great peril. But my fate was not
sealed.
Then the noble prince, Healfdene's son,
rewarded me generously with valuable gifts.

BOOK XXIX

76 THIS KING WAS DEVOTED to old traditions,
and I lacked nothing in the rewards I received,
acknowledging my strength. Gifts were bestowed upon me
by Healfdene's successor, to use as I pleased.
Now, my prince, I offer them all to you,
eagerly giving them. Your favor alone
can grant me acceptance. I have few,
if any, relatives, except you, Hygelac!"
Then he instructed them to bring him the boar-head standard,
the tall battle helmet, and gray chestplate,
the magnificent sword; and he spoke formally:
"This war equipment was given to me by the wise old prince,
Hrothgar, and he commanded
that its tale be told to you immediately.
For a time, it belonged to Heorogar, the king,
who ruled the land of the Scyldings,
but he did not pass it down to his son,
courageous Heoroweard, despite his affection,
his armor for battle. Safeguard it well!"

I also heard that following this, he gifted
four fine apple-fallow horses and weapons,
each one identical, to the king.
This is how it should be among relatives,
not plotting betrayal against each other,
or secretly planning death for a neighbor or comrade.
Hygelac and his nephew cherished each other deeply,
always looking out for the other's wellbeing.
I also heard that he presented a necklace to Hygd,
a remarkable treasure, which Wealhtheow, the king's daughter,
had given him.
He added three elegant, saddled horses to the gift.
Since receiving this present, the jewel shone brightly
on the queen's chest.
Thus, the son of Ecgtheow displayed his noble lineage.

77   KNOWN for his impressive accomplishments
        and honorable actions, he was not one to harm
        comrades or kin while drinking ale.
        His demeanor was not cruel,
        despite possessing the greatest strength
        among all sons of the earth,
        a glorious blessing bestowed by God
        upon this noble leader. For a long time,
        he was scorned and regarded as worthless
        by the Geatish warriors.
        The chief of clans often failed
        to show him favor at the feast.
        The strong men thought poorly of him,
        an unprofitable prince,
        but in the end, all his troubles found recompense.
        Then the noble earl commanded to bring forth
        a precious heirloom of Hrethel,

adorned with gold: no Geat had ever seen
a more magnificent sword.
He placed the weapon in Beowulf's lap
and granted him seven thousand hides,
along with a hall and high-seat.
They shared the ancestral land equally,
as well as their inheritance and home,
but the king was held in higher regard
due to his rule over the entire realm.
As years went by,
with terrible raids and ravages,
Hygelac and Heardred both fell in battle,
slain beneath the shield-wall by sword strokes,
when brave warriors from the Heatho-Scilfings,
overwhelming in arms, sought the young nephew of Hereric.
Then Beowulf ascended as king
to rule this vast kingdom,
and he governed it well for fifty winters,
a wise old prince,
protecting his land until the fateful night
when a Dragon awakened, wreaking havoc.
In a grave on a hill, the Dragon guarded a treasure
within a steep stone mound. A narrow path led to it,
Somehow, a person stumbled upon the hidden cave,
Unknown to all humans, it was a heathen's treasure trove.
When he entered, he noticed a glimmering golden goblet,
And without thinking twice, he took it in his hand.
Rather than returning it, he decided to steal it away,
Taking advantage of the sleeping guardian's negligence,
Little did he know that his action would bring terror upon
Not only himself, but also the prince and his people.

BOOK XXX

79   THAT's the path he took, against his own will,
In grave danger, toward the dragon's treasure.
Pressured by the perils of his role as a nobleman,
He fled in fear from the impending doom,
Seeking refuge as a sinful man.
He hesitated as he witnessed the horrifying sight,
His legs trembling, consumed by terror.
Yet, the wretched fugitive gathered his courage,
Pushed aside his fears, and swiftly departed,
Taking the cup from the hidden treasure.
In addition to that, there were plenty more,
Ancient heirlooms buried deep in the earth,
Left behind by some forgotten nobleman,
The last of his proud lineage,
Who carefully concealed them there,
Each one a precious treasure. Long ago,
Death had taken them all, leaving him alone,
The sole survivor of his clan,
Grieving for his friends, yet determined to stay,

Guarding the treasure, his only solace,
Despite the brevity of his respite.
The newly-prepared burial mound,
Stood near the strand and crashing waves,
Hidden and sealed by the nearby headland,
Within it lay his noble heirlooms,
And a vast hoard of heavy gold,
Protected by the guardian of precious rings.
He uttered few words, his voice choked with emotion:
"Now it is your turn, Earth, since heroes cannot,
To hold what noble warriors once possessed!
Brave men retrieved it from you long ago,
But they were slain in battle, their lives stolen,
Deprived of the joys of loyal service.
I have no one left to wield a sword,
Or to polish this magnificent cup,
A shimmering vessel of great value.
My brave comrades are gone,
And this boldly gilded helmet
Will soon lose its shine.
The craftsmen who once polished and adorned it,
Lie slumbering, unable to revive
The gleaming glory of this battle mask.
80   And those warriors, once fearless and brave,
Facing the clash of shields and sword's sharp bite,
Now lay rusted with their wearers' graves.
No more music from the harp, no joyous sounds,
No merry tunes from the wooden pipe.
No noble hawk flies through the silent hall,
No swift horses stamp in the city walls.
Battle and death have taken the young and brave,
Leaving behind sorrow and an empty race."
With a heavy heart, he mourned their loss,
Alone and sorrowful, he wept day and night,

Until the waves of death overcame his soul.
That hoard of happiness, the wicked dweller found,
The dragon who haunts the lonely tombs at twilight,
A fiery creature, spreading fear among men.
For centuries he guarded the heathen gold,
Seeking treasures in the graves, yet never gaining.
This scourge of the people, this powerful foe,
Kept watch over the hoard for three hundred winters,
Until one day, a furious rage ignited within him,
As a man approached with a precious cup, seeking peace.
Thus, the barrow was looted, its treasures taken away.
The poor man's request had been granted,
And his ruler witnessed the ancient creations of old.
When the dragon awoke, new sorrows arose.
He sniffed the air, searching for the scent
Of the enemy who dared to come so close.
May the unharmed ones easily escape
From evil and exile, if only they receive
The mercy of the Almighty! That guardian of gold.
He roamed over the land, driven by his greed
to find the one who had wronged him in his sleep.
Fierce and fiery, he circled the burial mound
all around, but found no one there,
no one in the desolate wilderness.... Yet he craved war,
eager for battle. He entered the barrow,
searching for the cup, and quickly realized
that a mortal had plundered his treasure,
his precious gold. The guardian waited
impatiently until evening arrived;
consumed by anger, he yearned to retaliate
with blazing flames for the loss of the beloved cup.
Now that the day had passed just as the dragon desired,
it was no longer content to remain by the mound's wall,

but soared through the air engulfed in fire:
a dreadful beginning for the dwellers of the land;
and soon, it brought a dreadful end
to their lord, sealed by his doom.

BOOK XXXI

82 Then the evil monster spewed its fire,
and bright homes were set ablaze. The flames rose high,
terrifying all the people. The loathsome creature
would not spare any living being as it flew overhead.
From far and wide, the dragon's destructive wrath
was witnessed, spreading fear and hatred
among the Geatish people. At the break of dawn,
it retreated to its hidden lair, to its treasure hoard.
The people in the land were burnt by its flames,
suffering from its evil and destruction.
The dragon believed its barrow and defenses
would protect it in battle, but it was a foolish pride!
The news of the calamity quickly reached Beowulf,
the king, whose magnificent hall, the best of buildings,
had been melted by the waves of fire, the great gift
from his people. The old ruler was filled with sorrow,
for he believed he had angered his sovereign God,
breaking the ancient laws and bringing bitterness
to the Lord. In his troubled heart, thoughts of darkness

swelled, something he had never experienced before.
The dragon had destroyed the fortress of the people,
washed away by flames and waves. But the valiant king,
leader of the Geatish warriors, planned his revenge.
He commanded his loyal followers, skilled in ironwork,
to craft a wondrous shield of war. He knew well
that wood from the forest was useless against fire,
and even the sturdy linden wood could not help.
As a brave prince, he knew his fate was sealed,
to end his fleeting life on earth, along with the dragon,
even though the beast had guarded its treasure hoard for long!
He considered it a shameful act, as a ring-giver,
to pursue the flying creature with a large force.
83 Beowulf led a large group; he wasn't scared of the battle,
nor did he find the dragon's fight too tough.
He had faced many desperate adventures and war dangers,
since he, a proud conqueror,
completely cleared Hrothgar's hall,
and in a fight killed Grendel's kin,
a horrible family! Especially memorable
was the close combat where Hygelac died,
when the leader of the Geats, in the heat of battle,
lord of his people, in Frisian territory,
Hrethel's son, was defeated by swords,
overpowered by enemies. From there Beowulf escaped
using his own strength and swimming skills,
alone, carrying thirty
suits of armor, when he reached the sea!
The Hetwaras, who fought against him
with their shields, couldn't proudly claim
their skill in battle: only a few survived
the fight with the hero and returned home!
Then Ecgtheow's son swam across the ocean,
alone and sad, going back to his country,

where Hygd offered him treasures, kingship,
rings, and the royal throne, not trusting
her own son's ability to protect their kingdom
from enemies after Hygelac's death.
The mournful people couldn't convince him
to be the lord and ruler over young Heardred,
but the hero supported him with kind words,
helping him honorably until he grew up
and ruled the Weder-Geats. Exiles,
Ohtere's sons, traveled across seas to find him.
84   He had rejected the rule of the powerful Scylfings' leader,
the strongest and most honorable warrior who shattered the chains,
in the land of Sweden, ruled by the sea-kings,
a proud hero. As a result, Heardred met his demise.
Although he offered them refuge, he was slain in battle,
struck down by the deadly edge of the sword, the son of Hygelac;
but the son of Ongentheow reclaimed his position,
seeking a new place to call home, after Heardred's fall,
leaving Beowulf as the ruler of the Geats
and the master of the noble throne. He was truly a remarkable king!

BOOK XXXII

85   To repay the loss of his lord, he desired,
in later days; and to Eadgils he became
a friend to the friendless, and sent
support over the sea to the son of Ohtere,
weapons and warriors: he was well rewarded
for those cold and difficult paths when he slew the king.
Thus, the son of Ecgtheow safely navigated
through numerous challenges and dire perils,
with bold and daring deeds, until this fateful day
that destined him to confront the dragon.
With eleven companions, the lord of Geats,
filled with anger, went in search of the dragon.
He had learned about the source of all the harm
and the killing of his people; the valuable cup
had been placed in the lord's lap by its discoverer.
Among the crowd was the thirteenth man,
the one who had started all the strife and troubles,
a captive burdened with worries; reluctantly
and under coercion, he led them

until they reached the sight of the cavern-hall,
the burial mound carved near the surging waves
of the ocean. Inside, it was filled
with valuable gold and jewels; a vigilant guardian,
a loyal warrior, held the treasures,
lurking in his lair. It was not an easy task
for any mortal to enter!
The hero king sat on the headland,
addressing words of greeting to his companions,
the Geats' trusted friend. His soul was heavy,
filled with uncertainty, nearing death. Fate was close
to welcome the aged man,
to take his life's wealth and separate
his spirit from his body. It would not be long
before the warrior's soul departed from his flesh.
Beowulf spoke, the son of Ecgtheow:
"Through countless struggles I fought in my youth,
I remember all the mighty feuds
I had encountered; each one comes to mind.
When I was just seven years old, the great king,
the protector of his people, took me from my father,
and Hrethel the king kept me close,
nourishing me with food and providing for me,
loyal in kinship. Never did he find me
more repulsive than his own sons,
Herebeald and Haethcyn, and even my own brother, Hygelac.
Unfortunately, due to a tragic accident
caused by Haethcyn, his own brother,
the eldest son met his death,
as Haethcyn mistakenly shot him down
with a fatal arrow that missed its intended mark,
taking the life of his own loyal lord
a fight without reason and a dreadful sin,
bringing horror to Hrethel. But, as difficult as it was,

the prince's death remained unavenged!
It is too unbearable for an old man
to witness his young child hang from the gallows.
He is left to compose a mournful poem,
a sorrowful song for his son that hangs there,
becoming a feast for ravens. The old man
knows there is no hope for rescue now,
as he himself is weak and powerless.
As the morning breaks, he still remembers
the heir who is no longer there; he does not hope
to see another successor to safeguard his wealth,
since the one who committed the deed
has met his own death. He looks upon
the empty halls of his son, the deserted mead-hall,
the chambers abandoned and swept by the wind,
stripped of all joyous celebrations.
The mighty warrior lies in deep slumber,
hidden far away; no harp plays its tunes,
no festive gatherings and toasts are heard in the halls, as they
once were.

BOOK XXXII

87   THEN HE GOES to his quarters, singing a mournful song
     alone for his lost son. Everything around him feels too big,
     his home and his possessions. The leader of the Weders
     kept his sorrow hidden in his heart for Herebeald,
     overwhelmed by waves of grief. He couldn't find a way
     to seek revenge for the heinous act of murder;
     nor could he even confront that hero
     with an act of disdain, though he didn't love him.
     And so, because of the suffering his soul endured,
     he gave up on happiness and chose the darkness of God.
     He left his lands and cities to his sons
     (as the wealthy do) when he passed away.
     There was strife and conflict between the Swedes and the Geats
     across the vast waters; war broke out,
     bringing dreadful battles, when Hrethel died,
     and Ongentheow's children grew up
     full of passion for strife, bold and unwilling
     to abide by a peace treaty across the seas,
     instead provoking their enemies

to launch attacks out of hatred from Hreosnabeorh.
My people sought revenge for that feud,
for the terrible war (as is widely known),
even though one of them paid for it with the blood of his heart,
a harsh sacrifice: for Haethcyn
met his fatal end in that battle, the first among the Geats.
In the morning, I heard, the murderer was killed
by a relative for the sake of family, with the clash of swords,
when Ongentheow faced Eofor in battle.
The war helmet split wide open: he fell, pale and lifeless,
the aged Scylfing; the hand that struck him
didn't forget about their feud and didn't hesitate with the fatal
blow.
"For all that he had given me, my shining sword
repaid him in war, such was the power I wielded,
for noble treasures: he entrusted me with his lands,
his home and his possessions. He didn't need
anything from the Swedish realm, or from the people of Spear-
Danes.
or from people of the Gifths, to get him help,
some warrior worse for pay to hire!
Always I fought at the front of all,
alone in the forefront; and so shall I fight
as long as I live and this blade shall last
that has proved loyal early and late
since the day Daeghrefn fell, slain by my hand,
the Hugas' champion.
He did not return from there to the Frisian king
with the loot and the prized adornments;
but, killed in battle, that brave nobleman
fell, brave prince. He was not killed by a sword,
but his bones were crushed by a strong grip,
his heart silenced. Now the sword-edge,
hard blade and my hand, shall strive for the treasure."

Beowulf spoke, and made a final battle vow:
"I have lived through many wars in my youth; now once again,
I, the defender of the old people, will seek a feud,
perform mighty deeds, if the dark destroyer
comes forth from his cave to fight me!"
Then he hailed all the helmeted heroes,
greeting his dear companions in battle for the last time:
"I should not bring any weapon,
no sword to fight the serpent, if only I knew
how, against such an enemy, I could regain
my courage as I did in Grendel's day.
But I must fear fire in this fight,
and poisonous breath; so I bring with me
a breastplate and a shield. I will not retreat
from the keeper of the barrow. One battle shall end
our war at the wall, as fate determines,
the master of all mankind. My spirit is brave
but refrains from boasting about this battling flyer."
Now, warriors in armor, stay near the burial mound,
wearing your breastplates, as we must await
the outcome of this battle. It is not for you
to fight, but for me alone to face
this monster and play the role of hero.
I will courageously win that treasure,
or it will be a cruel fate that takes
your king and lord through deadly violence!"
The brave champion stood up, shield in hand,
relying on his own strength and courage,
and boldly approached the cave, wearing his helmet
and armor under the cliff's cleft he was no coward!
He soon spotted an arched stone by the wall,
and within it, a stream that flowed
from the burial mound. The water was hot with fire.
He knew he couldn't reach the treasure unharmed,

nor endure the depths due to the dragon's flames.
Filled with rage, the prince of the Geats
let out a fierce cry from his chest;
his voice echoed beneath the gray rocks.
The dragon heard the sound of a human voice
and became even more enraged. There was no turning back
from the pact of peace! The foul creature unleashed
its poisonous breath from the cave,
filling the air with a foul stench of battle.
The brave king raised his shield by the stone path,
defending himself against the loathed dragon,
while the coiled foe, filled with rage,
approached, seeking a fight. The strong king
pulled out his sharp sword, ready for battle.
90 Now gather around the burial mound, you warriors in armor,
Which one of us will emerge victorious from this battle?
Wait and see. This fight does not concern you all,
But only me, the one who will challenge this monster,
And play the role of the hero. I will bravely
Win that treasure, or else death will claim
Your king and lord in a cruel killing!
Up stood the brave champion, holding his shield firmly,
Relying on his strength and courage,
And wearing his armor beneath the cliffs—no cowardly route!
The warrior chief soon spotted an arch of stone near the wall,
A survivor of many victorious battles
Where enemies clashed fiercely.
Inside was a stream flowing out of the burial mound,
Its waters boiling with fire. He knew
He couldn't approach the treasure unharmed
Or endure the depths due to the dragon's flames.
Filled with rage, the prince of the Geats
Couldn't hold back his words any longer.
He yelled angrily, his cry echoing

Beneath the gray cliff rocks for all to hear.
The guardian of the treasure heard a human voice
And became enraged. There would be no peace now,
No opportunity for negotiations!
The foul worm emerged from the cave,
Breathing out its poisonous fumes, filling the air
With the stench of battle. The rocks shook.
The Geatish king raised his shield,
Standing strong against the monstrous abomination,
While the coiled foe approached, seeking a fight.
The brave king drew his sharp sword,
Not dull or worn, but a precious heirloom,
And both combatants felt a sense of fear,
Despite their fierce intentions.
The warrior king held his shield high,
Shielding his body and soul,
But it wouldn't last long enough
To satisfy his desire for victory.
Fate denied him that respite,
And the glory of winning. He swung his arm,
Striking the fierce enemy with his noble sword,
But the blade turned dull and weak
As it hit the dragon's tough scales.
The guardian of the mound grew furious
At that powerful blow, and unleashed
Deadly flames that spread far and wide.
The Geatish lord couldn't boast of victory,
His sword failing him in battle,
Leaving him defenseless,
When it should have served him well
With its exceptional iron! Now he faced
A difficult path, Ecgtheow's honored heir,
Across the field towards the enemy,
Forced to find another home,

Far away, like all men,
Leaving this fleeting life behind!
It didn't take long before these fierce warriors clashed again,
The guardian of the treasure filled with renewed courage,
And the folk-commander found himself engulfed
In the flames of peril once more!
His comrades, the noble sons of kings,
Did not stand beside him with their weapons drawn,
But retreated to the safety of the woods.
they risked their lives to protect others,
But one of them had a heavy burden in his heart.
True family bonds cannot be broken
In the mind of someone honorable and kind.

BOOK XXXIV

92   Wiglaf was his name, the son of Weohstan,
     A beloved noble, of the Scylfings by blood,
     A relative of Aelfhere, with close kinship.
     He witnessed his king being fiercely attacked,
     Struggling beneath his helm, overwhelmed by the heat.
     He thought of the rewards his lord had bestowed upon him,
     The seat of honor from the Waegmunding clan,
     And the ancestral rights his father had possessed.
     He didn't hesitate for long. He grasped his yellow linden shield,
     And drew the ancient sword, a known relic:
     The same sword that had taken the life of Eanmund,
     Son of Ohtere, a friendless exile who met his end in combat,
     By the hand of Weohstan, who claimed as spoils
     The polished helmet and the ringed breastplate,
     The old sword of the Eotens, a gift from Onela,
     Armor of a brave warrior, battle-worn and bold.
     Although a relative had fallen in battle,
     Onela didn't feel the burden of their feud.
     Weohstan had kept this war-gear for many winters,

The breastplate and the shield, until his son was ready
To earn his own noble title, just as the old sire had.
Then, amidst the Geats, he bestowed upon him
The vast portion of battle-ready equipment,
Upon his passing, as he ventured into old age.
And now, for the first time, the young warrior
Stood alongside his leader-lord in the intensity of battle.
His spirit remained unyielding, not weakened by ancestral duty.
Thus, the dragon discovered this truth,
When the foes clashed together in fierce combat!
Wiglaf spoke, with wisdom in his words,
Grief-stricken, he addressed his comrades:
"I remember the time, as we drank mead,
The promise we made in the grand feasting hall,
To our ring-giver, our lord and protector,
To repay his generosity with our own valor in combat.
for swords and helmets, if fate should bring
such a challenging situation! Our leader chose us
from his entire army to assist him now,
he urged us towards glory and bestowed these treasures,
because he believed we were skilled with the spear
and courageous under helmets. Yet, he expected
to complete this heroic task unaided and alone,
as a defender of the people who has gained
more glory than any other man through bold deeds!
But now, the day has arrived
where our noble master needs the strength
of brave warriors. Let us march beside him
to lend our assistance while the battle rages,
intense and fierce! I swear by God as my witness,
I would much rather be consumed by the fire
alongside my lord than to return home
without having attempted to defeat the enemy
and defend the life of the Weders' lord.

It would be shameful, according to the laws of our land,
if the king alone among the Geatish warriors
endured suffering and perished in the struggle!
Both my sword and helmet,
breastplate and shield, will serve the two of us!"
Through the scent of bloodshed, he strode forward to help his leader,
holding his battle helmet, and spoke in few words:
"Dearest Beowulf, be brave and valiant,
as you vowed in your youthful days
that you would never let your glory fade
as long as you lived! Now, mighty in deeds,
hold firm, noble prince, and with all your strength
protect your life! I will stand by your side to assist you."
Upon hearing these words, the dragon attacked once more,
a furious and raging monster,
spewing flames in search of its enemies.
The men were despised. The sword-thane young
failed to shield himself as the flames devoured
his board and breastplate. But swiftly, he sought
refuge under his kinsman's shield,
since his own had been consumed by fire.
The fearless king, still mindful of his glory,
thrust his mighty sword into the dragon's head,
fueling his strike with hatred. But Naegling shattered,
Beowulf's sword broke in battle,
old and worn. It was not granted to him
that any iron edge could aid him at all
in the fight. His hand was too strong,
as the tale goes, and he swung too forcefully
with every sword he brandished,
no matter how sturdy their steel. They did not assist him.
For the third time, the fire-breathing dragon

recalled its vendetta against him,
and charged at the hero, wherever it could find space,
ferocious and blazing. Its sharp teeth
closed around Beowulf's neck,
covering him in a gush of blood from his wounded chest.

BOOK XXXV

95 Now, men say, in the time of need for his leader,
the noble earl revealed his noble lineage,
his skill, sharpness, and enduring courage.
Fearless of harm, although his hand was burned,
valiant-hearted, he aided his kinsman.
Lower down, he struck the repulsive creature
with his sword; his steel pierced through,
bright and polished; the fire started
to fade and diminish. Finally, the king
regained his composure, drew his war-knife,
a sharp blade hanging by his chestplate,
and struck the fiend, splitting it apart,
defeating the enemy, ending its life.
Thus they both killed it, two noble kinsmen,
two noble warriors: this is how an earl
should be on a day of danger! This victory
marked the end of the king's valorous deeds,
the culmination of his accomplishments in the world.
The wound, which the earth-dragon had inflicted,

started to swell and throb; soon he realized
a baleful and deep pain, the poison's effect,
boiling in his chest. The prince
wisely proceeded to the rocky wall;
there he sat and gazed at the massive structure,
the stone arch and sturdy pillar,
holding up that hall in the earth for eternity.
But now, the unparalleled servant's hand
must cleanse his beloved lord
with water, the king and conqueror covered in blood,
exhausted from battle, and remove his helmet.
Beowulf spoke, despite his injury,
his mortal wound; he knew well
that his time for earthly joy was over,
his days had all vanished,
and death was near:
"I wish to give to my son
This treasure of war, if it were given to me now,
to pass down to any heir that follows me,
of my own bloodline. I ruled over this people
for fifty long years. There was no king,
from any neighboring clans,
who would wage war against me, a friend of warriors,
and threaten me with terrors. I stayed at home,
awaiting my fate, and I cared for my own;
I did not seek feuds or make false oaths
ever. Despite being fatally wounded, I am eager
for all these things! The Ruler of Mankind
shall not be angry with me
when my life must depart from my body,
for the killing of kinsmen! Now go quickly
and look upon that treasure beneath the ancient rock,
beloved by Wiglaf, now that the dragon lies defeated,
resting, heart-sore, having been deprived of its spoils.

And go swiftly. I long to lay my eyes upon
the magnificent heirlooms, the golden wealth,
to take joy in the jewels and gems, and to
rest more peacefully, having seen this splendid treasure,
before I surrender my life and the lordship I have held for so
long."

BOOK XXXV

97 I HAVE HEARD that swiftly the brave son of Weohstan,
at the request and command of his wounded king,
his battle-worn body clad in a protective mail-coat,
carried beneath the burial mound's roof
a treasure-filled sack of wealth.
As this courageous clansman, proud of his victory,
passed by the royal seat, he beheld
a vast abundance of jewels and shimmering gold
scattered all along the ground;
marvelous items were strewn by the wall,
alongside numerous vessels inside the dragon's den,
the ancient flyer that appeared at dawn:
untarnished bowls once owned by long-gone men,
dull and worn helmets from times of old,
and many wonderfully crafted arm-rings.
Such a wealth of gold, plundered from the burial mound,
could fuel pride in any person;
let whoever desires hide it away! -
His gaze also fell upon a golden banner,

displayed high above the hoard, exquisitely embroidered;
its brightness was so intense that he could easily
see the entire floor of the earth and all the vessels.
No trace of the serpent was visible at that moment:
the sword had taken care of it.
Then, I heard, the hill was stripped of its treasures,
the ancient works of giants, by this lone hero;
he filled his bosom with beakers and plates
at his own choosing, and took possession of the flag,
the most dazzling of the beacons. -
With its sharp iron edge, the sword of his lord
had inflicted deep wounds
upon the guardian of the golden hoard,
who had protected it for many years.
The fiery breath of the dragon
had spread terror-filled waves of heat
around the barrow in the midnight hour,
until it met its doom.
The herald hurried, spurred by the treasure,
as he retraced his steps, while troubled by doubts,
the high-spirited hero, uncertain if he would find
his lord, the king of the Weders, where he had left him, still alive.
He quickly weakened by the cave's wall.
So he carried the burden. He found his lord and king,
bleeding and renowned, near death.
The loyal servant splashed him with water
until he regained consciousness. Beowulf spoke,
wise and sorrowful, as he stared at the gold.
"I give thanks to God and the Mysterious Maker,
for what I see, and to the Lord of Heaven,
for the grace of being able to bestow such gifts upon my people
before the day of my death arrives!
Now I have exchanged my life for this treasure,
so take good care to tend to the needs of my land!

I will not stay any longer. Prepare a burial mound,
raised by those who were inspired by the battle,
near the flowing river, standing tall on Hrones Headland,
so that sailors may often greet
Beowulf's Monument, as they return
from faraway lands, sailing over the dark waves."
He unclasped the gold collar from his neck,
the brave king, and handed it to his loyal vassal,
along with a shining golden helmet, breastplate, and ring,
and commanded him to use them with joy.
"You are the last remaining descendant of our noble lineage,
the last bearer of the Waegmunding name.
Destiny has taken all my kin
to the land of the dead, glorious men:
and I will follow them."
This was the last thought that the wise old man
held in his heart, before he chose
the burning waves of death as his fate.
His soul left his body
to seek the reward of the saints.

BOOK XXXVII

99 IT WAS a heavy blow for the young hero
to see his beloved lord lying lifeless on the ground,
a sorrowful sight. But the fearsome dragon,
that venomous creature, also lay defeated,
deprived of breath. It could no longer
possess its hoard, for sharp iron weapons
brought its end, struck by mighty hammers.
Silenced by its wounds, it fell to the ground
near its treasure, no longer able
to soar through the midnight sky,
proudly displaying its spoils. It succumbed
to the hero-king's skillful handiwork.
Indeed, only a few among men--
however strong and valiant, as the tales tell,
never lacking in boldness and bravery--
dare to face the deadly fumes of a poisonous foe
and charge into the perilous realm of the foe's lair,
while the guardian watches over the hall.
Beowulf paid the ultimate price

for that precious treasure;
both he and the dragon met their end
in that fleeting moment of life.
Soon after, the cowards and deserters,
ten men in total, who had abandoned the battle,
fearing to wield a spear in defense
of their noble lord in his great distress,
returned in shame, carrying their shields and armor,
to where the old man lay. Their eyes then turned
to Wiglaf. Exhausted, he sat
beside his king, a loyal defender,
attempting to revive him with water. But it was in vain.
No longer could he preserve the life
of his esteemed leader in this world.
The will of all-powerful God cannot be thwarted,
His decrees govern the actions of every person, even today.
A stern response was readily given
to those who succumbed to fear, from the valiant youth!
Wiglaf, son of Weohstan, spoke,
his gaze mournful as he looked upon those unfaithful men.
"Those who speak the truth can attest
that the king who bestowed upon you golden rings
and the armor in which you now stand,
for he oftentimes bestowed helms and breastplates
to his loyal subjects at the ale-bench,
from near or far, seeking to give them
the finest gear he could find.
And yet you wasted and discarded these weapons of battle,
when the enemy arrived and you failed!
The king could not boast of his comrades-in-arms,
even though the Almighty God, the Victorious Protector,
granted him grace by enabling him
to avenge his enemies solely with his sword,
in times of stress and desperation.

In the struggle, I could do little
to save his life, but I made an effort
(hopeless as it seemed) to support my kinsman.
Each blow I landed weakened the enemy,
and the fire within him burned less brightly.
Yet too few heroes came forward
to aid our king in his trial!
Now, the gifts of treasure and the security of swords,
which brought joy to our home and people,
shall be lost to you. Every member of your kin,
within your clan, shall abandon and forsake
your ancestral land, when noble lords
far and wide hear of your disgraceful retreat,
an infamous deed. Yes, death is preferable
for loyal subjects than a life of shame!"

BOOK XXXVIII

101 THAT ARDUOUS BATTLE COMMANDED AN ANNOUNCEMENT,
at the fort on the cliff, with great sorrow,
where the mighty warriors had sat all morning,
brave shield-bearers, uncertain of two outcomes:
would they mourn him as dead or welcome him home,
their beloved lord? Few details were withheld,
as the messenger who rode up the hill
revealed the news to them all.
"Now the generous giver to the people of Weder
lies on his deathbed; the Lord of Geats
sleeps on the battlefield, slain by the serpent!
And beside him lies the killer of men,
wounded by knife thrusts, but no sword
could harm that fearsome creature in any way.
There sits Wiglaf, son of Weohstan,
by Beowulf's side, a living warrior
next to the deceased,
and with a heavy heart, he keeps vigil
over friend and foe. Now our people should expect

a war to be waged, as news of the king's demise
spreads far and wide to the Frisians and Franks.
The conflict began
when Hygelac fell in battle against the Hugas
and journeyed with his fleet to Frisian lands.
There the Hetwaras humbled him with their might,
overwhelming his power
and causing him to perish in combat.
That noble lord could not reward his loyal followers!
Since then, the favor of the Merowings has completely failed us.
I have no expectations of peace and trust
from the people of Sweden. It was widely known
how Ongentheow deprived Haethcyn Hrethling
of hope and life at Ravenswood,
when the Geats, in reckless pride, first encountered
the warlike Scylfings."
102   The old and wise Ohtere fought back,
defeating the powerful sea-king,
and saving his wife, though her gold was stolen.
She was a mother to Ohtere and Onela.
Then, he pursued his fleeing enemies,
who were in a desperate situation,
and cornered them at Ravenswood.
He besieged them with his army,
threatening them with further suffering,
throughout the long night.
Some would be killed by his sword in the morning,
while others would be hanged on the gallows,
left for ravens to feast upon.
But as the dawn broke, salvation arrived for those men,
as they heard the sound of Hygelac's horn,
his trusted king had followed their path,
accompanied by a faithful band.

BOOK XXXIX

103   THE FIERCE BATTLE between the Swedes and Geats
was seen from afar, the clash of their swords.
The old king and his noble warriors
sought refuge in the citadel, filled with sorrow.
Earl Ongentheow went up to his fortress,
having tested Hygelac's bravery before,
no longer daring to defy those warriors,
nor hoping to save his treasure, child, and wife.
He returned to his walls, old and tired,
but Hygelac's army pursued him,
slaughtering the Swedes as they advanced with pride
across the peaceful plains, until they reached
the fortified town where the Hrethelings fought.
There, the hoary-bearded Ongentheow
was held back by the sword's edge,
forced to endure the anger of Eofor.
In retaliation, Wulf Wonreding struck
the king with his weapon, causing
the chieftain's blood to flow beneath his hair.

But the brave Scylfing felt no fear,
swiftly striking back with a better blow,
facing his enemy with fierce determination.
However, the son of Wonred was not quick enough
to defend against the aged chief's attack,
his helmet was cleaved too soon,
and he fell to the ground, covered in blood.
Though wounded, he was not yet defeated,
growing stronger despite the pain.
Then, one of Hygelac's loyal warriors
struck with a mighty sword, shattering the giant's helmet,
breaking through the shield-wall.
The king sank to the ground,
His people's elderly caretaker, gravely wounded.
Many rushed to attend to the injured brother,
supporting him as quickly as fate allowed
to bring him to the battleground.
But Eofor seized from Ongentheow,
the noble earl, his heavy breastplate,
his sword with a sturdy hilt, and his helmet,
and brought the old king's armor to Hygelac,
who accepted the spoils and generously promised
a generous reward among his people, and he kept his word.
As a result of that fierce battle, the Geatish lord,
descendant of Hrethel, returned home
and bestowed a wealth of treasure upon Eofor and Wulf.
Each of them received a hundred thousand
in land and valuable rings, for such heroic acts
were highly esteemed by the people.
To Eofor, he also gave his daughter
as a sign of gratitude, a source of pride in his home.
"This is the vendetta, the enemy's wrath,
the lethal hatred of men. It is certain
that the Swedish people will seek revenge

for the fall of their friends, the fighting-Scylfings,
once they discover that our valiant leader
lies lifeless, he who defended our land and wealth,
fostered the prosperity of our people, completed his journey
as a courageous hero. Now, the sooner the better,
let us go and pay our respects to our Geatish lord,
and carry the generous ring-giver
to his funeral pyre. No mere fragments
shall burn with the warrior. All the precious jewels,
untold gold obtained through warfare,
the treasure he acquired during his lifetime,
the flames shall consume. No nobleman shall wear
a keepsake. No fair maiden shall possess it.
105 No maiden fair shall wear noble rings,
with sorrow in her heart and without gold.
She will travel the path of exile,
now that our lord has abandoned laughter,
mirth, and revelry. The warriors,
in the cold morning, will grasp their spears,
lift them high; no melodic harp
shall awaken these warriors,
but the pale raven, eager for the fallen,
will feast and boast to the eagle
about how bravely he ate while he and the wolf devoured the
slain."
 So he shared his sorrowful news,
speaking the truth, the loyal man,
both in word and in action. The warriors arose;
with tears streaming, they ascended the Cliff-of-Eagles,
to witness the astonishing sight.
There, on the sand, laid to rest,
was their lifeless lord, who had generously bestowed rings
upon them in the past. The day had come to an end,
and death had taken hold of the valiant king of the Weders.

Besides their fallen leader,
they also saw a peculiar creature,
loathsome and lying nearby,
stretched out on the battlefield. The fiery dragon,
a fearsome fiend, had been scorched by flames.
It measured fifty feet in length as it lay there.
Once, it had reveled during the night and returned,
seeking its den. Now, in the grip of death,
it had reached the end of its earthly joys.
Beside it, there stood vessels and jars;
dishes were scattered, and adorned swords
were consumed by rust, lying on the earth's surface,
having waited there for a thousand winters.
The immense wealth, the gold of the past,
was trapped under a mystical spell.
106 Thus, the treasure-hall was inaccessible
to all mortals, except for one
chosen by the divine King of Heaven,
God Himself, who could grant permission
to whom He deemed worthy,
the Champion of Heroes, to unlock the hoard,
a man who appeared suitable in His eyes.

BOOK XL

107 A TREACHEROUS PATH IT WAS, he walked upon
concealing himself within the hidden hall,
where wealth was hidden beneath the walls!
The guardian of the treasure had slain one of the few,
avenging a feud in a sorrowful manner.
It is remarkable how a man of strength and courage
often ends his life, when the noble lord
can no longer live in the mead-hall
amongst his beloved friends.
So when Beowulf sought out the guardian
of the barrow and engaged in the struggle,
he himself did not know how he would ultimately
depart from this world.
The mighty princes, who placed the gold,
covered it deeply with a curse until Doomsday,
so that the person who dared to steal their treasure
would be marked with sin,
bound tightly in hellish chains,
tormented by afflictions.

But the king's view was not driven by greed for gold,
but rather the grace of heaven.
Wiglaf, the son of Weohstan, spoke up:
"Often at the command of one, many warriors
must suffer sorrow, and so must we.
The beloved king showed no regard
for our advice, the people's shepherd!
We urged him not to engage with that
guardian of gold, but to let him rest
where he had been for so long,
in his underground hall, awaiting the end of the world,
as decreed by heaven. This hoard is now ours,
but it was obtained through great suffering;
the fate that led our king and lord there
was too cruel. I was inside, and I saw it all,
the chambered treasure, when circumstances permitted me
(and the path I took was not at all pleasant)
under the earth-wall. I eagerly took
as much of the treasure as my hands could carry
and quickly brought it back here."
108   To my noble lord and liege, he was still alive,
his mind still sharp. The wise old man
spoke with great sadness and sent you his greetings,
asking that when he no longer breathes,
you build a lofty mound on the site of his funeral pyre,
a mighty memorial. Among men, he was
the greatest warrior throughout the wide world,
while he delighted in his treasures and stronghold.
Now let us set forth quickly, for a second time,
to see and explore this hidden treasure hoard,
these marvelous wonders hidden within the walls--I will guide
you--
where, gathered together, you may gaze
to your heart's content at the vast amounts of gold and rings.

Prepare the funeral pyre and have everything ready
for when we return to carry our beloved king and leader
to his resting place, where he shall dwell for a long time
in the safety of the sovereign God."
Then the brave son of Weohstan commanded
many heroes, owners of their homesteads,
to bring firewood from afar, over their lands,
for the funeral of the renowned hero. "The fire shall consume
and pale flames shall feed on the fearless warrior
who often stood strong in the iron rain,
when a barrage of arrows, swiftly shot from bows,
flew over the shield wall--the arrows held firm,
skillfully feathered, following the shaft."
And now the wise young son of Weohstan
selected seven of the chief's loyal warriors,
the best he could find among that group,
and together with these warriors, he ventured,
one of eight, into the hostile hall. One of them carried
a lit torch and led the way.
No lots were cast for dividing the treasure
once the warriors saw it in the hall.
Completely unguarded it lay there,
left abandoned without a care.
No sorrow was felt as they hurriedly dragged,
that precious treasure, so dearly snagged!
The dragon they threw, the serpent, o'er the wall,
to be consumed by the waves' swift call.
The crashing water swallowed up with ease,
that shepherd of gems, entrapped in the seas.
Then the woven gold was loaded onto a cart,
countless in number, every part!
And the king was carried, so aged and bold,
to Hrones-Ness, where his story would unfold.

BOOK XLI

110 THE PEOPLE of Geats then built a funeral pyre
for their beloved leader, firm on the ground.
They adorned it with helmets and war equipment,
bright breastplates, fulfilling his final request.
They placed the mighty chieftain among it,
while heroes mourned their dear master.
On the hill, the largest of funeral fires
was lit by the warriors. Smoke rose,
darkening the sky, blending with the sound
of flames and weeping (the wind stood still),
until the fire consumed the bones,
burning hot at the core. In their heavy hearts,
they moaned, burdened by their grief and loss.
The old widow, with bound hair,
sang a mournful song for Beowulf's death,
expressing her sorrow and fearing
the days to come, filled with more deaths,
battle and shame. The smoke was swallowed by the sky.
The people of Weders then built a broad and tall

burial mound on the headland,
visible to sailors far out at sea.
In just ten days, they completed their task,
raising a beacon for the brave warrior.
Around the pyre's ashes, they constructed a wall,
the most remarkable design ever crafted
by their wisest men. They placed inside the mound
the precious treasure, the rings and plunder
seized by courageous heroes from the cave,
entrusting it to the earth where it rests,
useless to men, as it has been for ages.
A group of twelve noble-born warriors
circled the mound, riding with grief,
chanting dirges, honoring their fallen leader.
They spoke highly of his leadership, his courageous deeds,
truly witnessed and deserving of praise.
It is fitting that people wholeheartedly celebrate
and sincerely love their respected friend and ruler
when he departs this life, leaving behind only his body.
So the people of Geatland mourned,
grieving for the loss of their heroic leader.
They declared him the gentlest and most beloved
among all the kings in the world,
the kindest to his family and most eager for recognition.